The Art and Science of Intergalactic Warmongery

The Art and Science of Intergalactic Warmongery

Field Marshal S. Myrston

COSMIC
EGG
BOOKS

Winchester, UK
Washington, USA

First published by Cosmic Egg Books, 2016
Cosmic Egg Books is an imprint of John Hunt Publishing Ltd., Laurel House, Station Approach,
Alresford, Hants, SO24 9JH, UK
office1@jhpbooks.net
www.johnhuntpublishing.com

For distributor details and how to order please visit the 'Ordering' section on our website.

ISBN: 978 1 78535 163 1
Library of Congress Control Number: 2015939705

A CIP catalogue record for this book is available from the British Library.

Design: Stuart Davies

Printed in the USA by Edwards Brothers Malloy

We operate a distinctive and ethical publishing philosophy in all
areas of our business, from our global network of authors to
production and worldwide distribution.

CONTENTS

1. Introduction

My first invasion, let's start with that. There was a planet somewhere beneath the grey soup we were falling through. I, the beloved leader of the Molagrian Empire, was leading the invasion. My entire armada was in formation behind me, taking a beating from the plasma flack the locals were firing in a feeble attempt to discourage us.

Finally it was happening. I'd been planning for over two years. Building up the military from scratch, squeezing money out of widows and capitalists and making promises for the rest. Haggling with roboticists and generals endlessly over the best way to take the planet. And then, the very moment the engines cut out and we started falling, it was all worth it. I remember a feeling washing over me. Transcendence. Omnipotence.

You're going to love it; all systems armed and each city allocated to your legions, every defensive structure set to be destroyed by orbital bombardment in the next few minutes. Your troopers, bundled into their dropping pods, clutching their ion rifles like talismans in the darkness and falling into that heavy gravity, each one eager to taste the blood of your enemy. It was wonderful. Hell, I have an erection even as I'm dictating this to my secretary. She looks uncomfortable. This is awkward now.

Moving on. The initial attack isn't even the best part of an invasion. Not for me, my favorite part comes later, when you've decimated the adversary and the planet's gone quiet. You've got the drones out, hunting down the errant antagonists still in hiding. Your forces have killed the Praetorian Guard and pulled back on your orders; allowing you the honor of walking up the stairs to the emperor's bedroom where you can lovingly wrap your tentacles around his head. And then, simply squeeze the life from him.

The Cardonian emperor was still wearing his pajamas when I

1

found him. That's a pretty good indicator of how surprised he was with our arrival. They were so soft and squishy, those Cardonians. I used to hug my hatchlings harder when saying goodnight to them.

While listening to the sound of his heart failing, a pretty melody if there ever was one, off in the distance I could hear the occasional plasmatic drone fire. I remember thinking that I was truly happy for the first time in my life. That was a good moment. I've done it again of course, hundreds of times, but that first one was...it was just special. It was like drawing my first breath after a lifetime of suffocating.

Nothing else in your life will ever measure up, not your first act of chemical genocide, or even intercourse with a living and willing participant. It's the single finest moment any being can hope to achieve as a mortal in this universe. And I can give it to you; if you want it badly enough; if you're willing to take my word as gospel and eschew that moralistic bullshit you've been preprogramed to believe that you believe in.

You need to do more than just simply read this book. You need to study it, absorb it: considering every point offered within. For if you master these battle-tested strategies, you can start a life dedicated to intergalactic warmongering. And what a life that will be.

2. Taking Control

There are those who seem to be content with life, who accept what God, chance and a flawed society have deemed to be their station in the universe. A true warmonger is never going to accept that fate. Not unless the position offered is that of Emperor, and his empire stretches for light millennia in every direction. Even then, that might not suffice to assuage his appetite for exploration, power and wealth.

In every generation, on every planet, there's at least one warmonger born, hatched, assembled or bubbled into existence with an ambition stretching to the stars. If you've ever found yourself staring into the night sky and, unlike your brethren beside you who are contemplating their own insignificance, you find yourself renaming star clusters and removing others, you could very well be one of us, a warmonger, God-king, Emperor, or Space-Tyrant.

Psychiatrists and similar charlatans have always labelled our kind as megalomaniacs, sociopaths or narcissists. But allowing those hacks to judge us is like asking the blind to name birds that don't sing. Their incapacity to comprehend our greatness leaves them no option but to conclude we suffer from some form of insanity. They'll never grasp our purpose, our potential, for how could they?

Our place is in the stars, in front of legions armed and trained to execute our every whim. Theirs is a quiet room, a dull conversation and faith in dead texts written by strange men who never cared for the scientific method. Well pish tosh, I say to them.

There are several standard routes available to achieving dominance of your species. Most of them require a lifetime of servitude and political kowtowing. By the time you achieve your goal of supremacy with this method, you'll be too old to invade the canteen of the retirement home you've been banished to. The normal route to the top reads like this: Be born to a well-respected family, get good grades at school and work your way up the postal services until you hit forty, then try your hand at local politics, gradually growing a support base, until you take local leadership, then continental controller and then, if lucky, become Emperor. This is no route for a warmonger. Instead, below are a few options you may wish to consider:

2.1 Ascension Techniques

2.1.1 Be born to it. Even in democracies, the electorate generally aren't sufficiently intelligent to weigh up the best candidate based on their policies and track record. Besides, if your democracy is older than twenty years, they've already figured out what candidates say to get elected in no way relates to what they actually do once in office. The voting population of most planets will choose somebody whose name is familiar to them. So if you have a father and a brother who have been president in the past, you're probably going to be elected even if you're an obese baldy without earlobes, who spends his days stroking cats and laughing maniacally with an exotic accent.

2.1.2 Secret Societies. Ask around about what secret societies are available and take advantage of their influential abilities. Choose carefully because many secret societies were only created to allow middle aged men to spank the naked bottoms of younger men, without the moment being awkward. They have all failed in this regard, it's always awkward. That being said, some of these cults and self-help networks can prove indispensable in your clamoring journey to power. Some can offer money, others will help with judges and officials and even vote tampering. So go ahead and learn the handshakes, the silly names, rituals and symbols. Just remember, as a rule, if during your induction ritual, you find your underwear around your ankles, you've probably made the wrong choice.

2.1.3 Write a book espousing wonderful principles. Write it in prison if possible. Speak of a great destiny with a prosperous future and living space aplenty. Make it seem reasonable and achievable, though it isn't either. If it's a sufficiently utopian fantasy, the electorate will take a shine to you. Follow through by running for office or forming your own party, based on your principles of love, peace and military ingenuity, coupled with lightning fast attacks to liberate ancient provinces who speak languages vaguely similar to your own.

2.1.4 Kiss babies. Never underestimate how effective charisma can be in a campaign. Kissing babies and singing well does wonders for one's political aspirations. The average housewife will sooner vote with the moist patch between her legs before considering the administrational abilities of any candidate. Similarly, for men, they will vote for someone who looks like them, talks like them and rolls up his sleeves occasionally to create an impression of familiarity.

An important part of politics lies in the ability to say things that people want to hear and nothing else. Any refined incumbent will never talk about conscription, corporate ownership of politicians or taxes, except to recite a rehearsed sound bite when pushed hard on the subject. Instead they will pick some arbitrary, irrelevant topic and speak to that, like gay marriage, flag burning or abortion. In the next sentence they'll praise the country's commitment to freedom.

2.1.5 Religious Overthrow. Be pious, be a prophet, be an avatar, hell, be a god if you want. Take control of any cult or religion and adjust it to suit your purposes. Use words like heretic and apostate when burning your competition and you'll probably get away with it. Be sure to wear robes and garish religious symbols.

If you have access to advanced technology, use it to fake miracles. Once your cult is firmly established within society it's a quick step from pope / rabbi / imam to emperor with a god backing you.

2.1.6 Unite the Clans. A very popular means of rising to power in ancient times involved taking control of a small, aggressive tribe and using them to attack and assimilate others into your kingdom. Once you've taken your first few clans, you should be big enough to intimidate newcomers into joining your burgeoning empire without fighting. Don't worry, as you continue to expand your borders you will still encounter kingdoms unwilling to surrender. Practitioners of this sort of state spend most of their lives campaigning. The very best of these leave a world forever changed by their warmongering, often forging countries and well-established infrastructures where before there were nothing but dirt tracks and skinny nomads bickering over yaks and cattle.

2.1.7 Subvert the media and pollsters to call election results and popularity ratings in your favour. Most of the voting public are sheep and like to vote for the incumbent who is likely to win. It's a bit of a chicken and egg scenario which can hatch success if manipulated correctly.

2.1.8 Promise what you can't deliver. Promise to cure cancer, invent a new color, eliminate poverty or offer endless, single-malt whiskey from a Scottish distillery that doesn't exist. Your opponent is telling porky pies too, just crappy ones about growth rates and fiscal stability, so why not make yours better and bigger? It shows ambition and vision for the future. Once you take office you can have all the promises redacted from your manifesto and introduce taxes and conscription like you were always going to.

2.1.9 Tyrannicide. There is a legal and moral precedent acknowledging a civilian's right to kill a tyrant. I'll be honest with you, the emperor's guardsmen probably aren't going to debate this with you while you're holding a bloodied dagger in the throne room. They're just going to kill you violently. In ancient Greece, Rome and Catholic philosophy they go even further than simply claiming tyrannicide can be tolerated in certain cases, to proclaiming it as the duty of every citizen to protect the will of the people. So if the current leader has changed his title to 'Beloved Supreme Leader' or altered his presidential term from four years to forever, then you might just get away with killing him legally. If the man is hated by the people, you could very well take his place. Earth's Benjamin Franklin proposed this motto for the Great Seal of the United States: "Rebellion to Tyrants is Obedience to God." Sure, he didn't say kill anyone, but you get where he was going with it. Obviously, when you take power, this sort of insurrectional propaganda needs to be stamped out and quickly.

2.1.10 Eat the leader and assume his identity. Perhaps less intricate than other power strategies, it is very often the quickest solution. If you are capable of shapeshifting, then it should be no problem at all, if not, consult plastic surgeons, scientists and aliens in hiding for the required science. You don't have to actually eat the emperor if you don't want to, but you do need to get rid of the body permanently. You should also be able to speak like the victim, using similar mannerisms and quirks. His aides and friends will become suspicious if he suddenly changes his diet, vocabulary, or favorite prostitute. If you have a few close allies, have them assume the identities of his inner circle. It helps to have a friend to talk to for psychological, strategic and bragging purposes.

2.1.11 Mass Psychic Manipulation. There are several species capable of doing this. Some have limited ranges but I know of two planets with creatures who play in the minds of Earthlings as a pastime, not unlike how your teenagers play halo and WOW. Though they generally couldn't be bothered with meddling in politics, if you were to offer them a worthy sacrifice, I'm sure they'd happily influence the will of the voting public in your favour. The sacrifice will not be cheap but shouldn't amount to more than ten percent of the planet's goat population. There is also technology available which will allow you to implant dreams and nightmares into the minds of the electorate. This could easily be used to create an aversion for your competition or an illogical love for you. Speak to aliens – Daemons and Nebraxians in particular, and fringe scientists. If still unsuc-cessful, there's an Irish bar in the red light district of Amsterdam, next to the church that doesn't ring its bells anymore, which is frequented by Reticulans, speak to Birgit, she will point you in the right direction.

2.1.12 Rig the ballot. Old school but still effective. If votes are counted by electronic means, simply hack it, if tallied by hand, subvert the people in charge of counting. Intercept and replace ballot boxes. Manipulate opening and closing times. Change the voting age. Insist on identity documents with photographs; look at any factor which will play in your favour. Run out of ballot papers in zones you don't believe will weigh in favorably. Adjust the weather. Getting dirt on the head of the independent electoral commission never hurts.

2.1.13 The reluctant leader. A good transitional process for businessmen, scientists and military officers. First, you need to win over a couple of media moguls, senators or MPs. Use bribery, coercion or old-fashioned threats to get them talking about you. You will need to create or exploit some crises which the current leadership cannot resolve. Normally the crisis will be of your making, an active terrorist cell with a mortar in the capital will suffice. Have the mortar team start firing at random targets. It's not important who or what they hit as long as they remain active. At this point your media moguls and politicians should begin to speak publicly as if you are the only person who could solve the crisis. Make up a lie which seems plausible, i.e. your military experience, your understanding of the basic parabola. Let the problem linger for a while and then reluctantly agree to do it, in spite of your abhorrence for violence. Take a small team of police officials and hunt down the terrorists using the transponders you implanted beneath their skin and kill them all. You will be loved. You will be praised and when the next election rolls around, go ahead and reluctantly accept that nomination too.

2.1.14 Get dirt on the leader. Sleep with the king and make a sex tape while doing it, or if you're not his kind, then convince somebody pretty to take one for the team and document that happening. If he's impotent or in love with his wife, then work with the president on a massive foreign arms-deal, which ensures his wealth becomes immeasurable, while the country takes ownership of outdated pieces of military hardware, which will now continue rusting, only on your corner of the planet as opposed to theirs. Then, once the deal is concluded, keep the contracts with the leader's signature and all the details of the junk. Take a photo of the Gripen jetfighters rusting in the hangers, the Corvettes floating like flotsam and use that evidence to convince the president to quietly stand down in the middle of his second term, or face scorn and ridicule from an electorate and prosecution from a judiciary he never got around to corrupting. Once you're in charge, get working on judges and prosecutors, set up a toothless enquiry, chaired by sycophants, and then delay the final outcome until everyone has forgotten about the incident or you're long dead.

2.1.15 Assassinations. Sure it's simple, even brutish, but if you've made it this close to the inner circle why not take the last few steps? Seventh-in-line to the throne is only one plane crash, or six shots away from you sitting in the pretty seat.

2.1.16 Sexual Congress. Sleeping with multitudes of women can guarantee you their votes if you do it properly. Take advantage of the willingness of females to talk to their friends and hairdressers about whom they've bumped genitalia against. Set yourself a daily target to achieve and establish a spreadsheet using identity numbers to keep track. If you sleep with five women a day, and the bragging ratio runs to one hundred and forty-three, which our latest research indicates it does, you will have two-and-a-half million faithful followers within ten years. Two-and-half million might not seem like a lot but these ladies will work tirelessly for you. This small core will actively and aggressively campaign for you. A loyal army like that can often prove to be the difference between becoming Emperor or Postmaster General. Also consider taking multiple wives if that's an option.

2.1.17 Mortal Combat. A lot of empires and kingdoms have a plethora of ancient by-laws that still exist legally but are never enforced. Take the time to have a lawyer read them for you to see if there's anything of value. I personally knew two kings and one head traffic official who took power by using the ancient laws that were still theoretically valid. One usurper challenged the reigning regent to a duel, another was able to have the ruler tortured for idolatry. As always, once you have exploited a rule to take power, be sure to abolish those old laws when you're in charge.

The above paths to power are by no means exhaustive, feel free to find your own or combine several as you see fit. Study your histories for ideas on how others have done it.

2.2 Decision Tree. The below diagram might help you decide which ascension method is best suited to your situation:

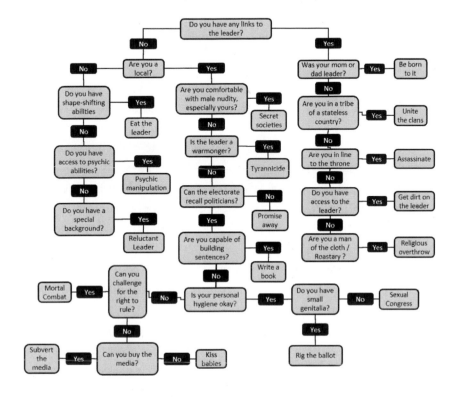

Figure 1. Decision Tree - Ascension Techniques.

3. Consolidating your Regime

So you have an empire. Congratulations. But what are you going to do with it? More importantly, how are you going to keep it? After all, you've just read seventeen ways in which power can pass to another and one of them worked for you, so never assume you are safe or entitled to your throne. Look at me, the living incarnation of the God-King of the Molagrian Empire, reduced to writing self-help books on a planet that could only be described as 'provincial.'

Taking your throne was probably the result of a bit of luck and daring, but holding on to it will require an unwavering vigilance, tireless administration and an unceasing paranoia you need to continuously nurture.

There are several different kinds of government available to a warmonger today. The system you recently inherited might not meet all your needs entirely, if so, have a look at the list below and select one which better suits you. Making the changes should be a matter for your lawmakers and chief of staff, it shouldn't take more than a week or two. Hell, if you do it properly, nobody needs to know about the switch to the despotic system you've selected.

3.1 Government types

3.1.1 Janus Democracy. On the surface, an enlightened society espousing the virtues of freedom, capitalism and minority protection. Beneath the surface it is a two-party system where both sides of the same coin take turns at the helm. Normally controlled by a group of wealthy individuals or corporations, where lobbying is both legal and encouraged. Financial systems are autonomously controlled by the funding corporations. Benefits include a large standing army with excellent technological capabilities and freedom from needing to worry about administrational duties. By selling the government controls and resources to the highest bidder you can raise massive amounts of cash in a short space of time. Politicians play an important role in any Janus democracy, for though they won't be able to do anything, they do need to give the impression that they are working to improve the lives of their people. They all need to be well versed in double-speak and corruptible beyond measure. The election process normally weeds out any honest and trustworthy individuals but sometimes an unruly individual will slip through. There are five ways, according to Sun Tzu, to ensure free-willed politicians conform; Those who are puritanical can be disgraced by whores and frauds (Berlusconi, Nixon); those who are ready to die for their cause can be assassinated in vehicular accidents or by high powered rifles (JFK, Nemtsov); those who are intent on living can be threatened into subservience or imprisoned (Mandela, North Korea, Tsvangirai); those who are quick to anger can be recorded losing their shit and then embarrassed (Brown); those who love people can be controlled by kidnapping or threatening loved ones (Navalny).

3.1.2 True Democracy. Democratic governments take care to ensure no one person or group can actually do anything of importance. They enjoy healthy academic arguments about what should be done and consider the debates to be sufficient. The will of the people is always taken into account, even if the majority, as pointed out by your Mr. Huxley, are foolish morons with no basic understanding of the complexities of government, defensive capabilities or the rule of law. I might have paraphrased that a bit. You need to read up on true democracy so you can convince your subjects that it is, in fact, the style of government they are currently enjoying.

3.1.3 Constitutional Monarchy. Pretty much a bog-standard

Janus democracy with the inclusion of an old lady sitting in a chair somewhere, lending legitimacy to your reign. The down side is she will insist on her face, or the visage of her favorite corgi, being used on all postage stamps and currency. The up side is she will make some of your speeches on your behalf. You get to enjoy Christmas while she does the talking. You can proof the language for political fuckups and grammar before she reads it. Modern examples include the United Kingdom, Japan, the Netherlands, and Qatar.

3.1.4 Communist State. In theory, the will of the people is given holy status in any communist state; luckily the will of the people is whatever you say it is and you don't even need to worry about the paperwork to prove it. All people are regarded as equal, except for you obviously, and any associates you deem special. Theoretically, no one person holds more property or food than they require. Education, health care, and pet insurance are all taken care of by the state. The government owns all the mines, businesses, vehicles and coffee shops in the land. The people work for the government. Everybody is happy. That's an order. A Lada is a wonderful car. Potatoes are a delicacy and more nutritional than steaks or hamburgers. The only problem with communism is, there is no incentive for civilians to start their own businesses or invent anything, so growth tends to stagnate regardless of all the whippings you dish out for encouragement. Current examples include: China, Cuba and Laos.

3.1.5 Anarchy. Some anarchists are drawn to the politics of chaos, finding it to be the only true weapon against the deceitful, self-serving politicians who use the masses as if slaves. Other anarchists are simply people who enjoy throwing bricks at coppers. In the midst of the chaos of a street protest, it's quite difficult to tell one type of anarchist from the other, so it's simplest to just kettle them all into a corner and then beat them into submission. Modern examples include Afghanistan and Yemen. Occasionally anarchy will rear its head for a few nights in developed countries, whenever local law enforcement shoots an unarmed member of a minority in the back with multiple rounds, in a brave act of self-defense. Protesters, believing the shooting was unintentional but still unacceptable take to the streets, once they realize law enforcement is quite willing to repeat the exercise on a massive scale, they tend to return to their homes.

3.1.6 Militaristic states are those nations which believe their ability to wage war is of paramount importance. They tend to militarize their society to a much higher degree than others and the tenants of the soldiers are widely shared by the civilians. They will always try to expand their borders into neighboring kingdoms, often taking slaves and resources as their own. While the nation continues to expand and conquer, the populations are generally happy and nationalistic. Once stagnation or defeat occurs though, the population will often turn against the leadership and burn them, not in effigy, but in person, on a stick, in someplace that's quite public. In a militaristic state, people who show prowess on the battlefield are awarded a higher status within the community. Training in the martial arts and firearms is a national obsession and sciences are structured around killing, maiming and expanding the empire. This really is an option worth considering. Modern examples include: North Korea, America and Russia.

3.1.7 Failed States. These are harder to pull off than you would imagine. Even in the worst governments, pockets of adequacy will emerge completely by chance. To achieve a failed state requires diligence and commitment. It's not a very popular choice for one's own empire but it's sure nice to see failure blossom across the border. It's also handy if you want to break down a government you can't corrupt from the inside, as it allows you to then use the "unite the clans" system to rebuild it to suit your purposes. Modern examples include Somalia, Yemen, Iraq and Pakistan.

3.1.8 Theocracies are generally reserved for those who took the throne through the religious overthrow method. It's a bit garish and over-the-top but if you pull it off, there are benefits far beyond those offered by democracies and similar systems. You need to convince the electorate of your divinity. The easiest way to achieve this is through mass hypnosis or a combination of psychedelic and euphoriant drugs. Others swear by using advanced or sly technologies, similar to stage magicians. Writing your own outlandish editorial pieces in newspapers doesn't hurt. Paying people to speak of the miracles witnessed goes a long way too. Modern examples include Vatican City and Iran.

3.1.9 Aristocracy is a system whereby a select few, who, due to the violent nature of their forefathers, enjoy the right to rule the throne as they see fit. No other people are deemed worthy of the title. Kings of old all enjoyed this daddy-based, blood-line system and it remains popular today. Swaziland, North Korea, Oman, Syria and Saudi Arabia are good modern examples of such a system. Interestingly, although the United Nations espouses democratic values, the permanent members of the Security Council enjoy "royal" status for their roles in a war that ended seventy years ago.

3.1.10 Digital Government. Probably the hardest system to subvert if implemented properly, digital governments are those which have the constitution and laws of the land programmed into a supercomputer. All the calculations and variables are available for public display and scrutiny. The full coding is open on a read only basis to the world. Referendums and election systems are integrated into this system. Never consider implementing this sort of government as you will find your hands tied by algorithms. Computer programmers and logicians will scrutinize the code and output systems regularly. If one of these systems exist in your government, burn it to the ground or turn the people against it by showing exceptions that are irrational. There are always exceptions that will result in loops or errors. The only official example on Earth is the Chilean Project, Cybersyn, from the seventies.

3.1.11 Hegemonic states are those controlled by another country or entity. The control can be as obvious or subtle as the situation allows. The hegemonic government's subservience is often the result of sycophantic politicians vying for favour with larger, more powerful entities. Sacrificing state controls for personal benefits or due to economic or military weaknesses of the puppet state. In today's political climate, with imperialism no longer popular, several states that have always been under the control of others now prefer a covert hegemonic relationship with their masters. Modern examples include Great Britain, Cuba, Surinam.

3.1.12 Autocratic states are those where a strong leader emerges by killing the previous throner, leading a rebellion or through a rigged election. They then proceed to cling to power through political maneuvering, legislative bullying and regular purging of politicians. These true warmongers take the throne and do what they want until they are killed violently by defenestration, stabbing in the chest repeatedly, or prostate cancer, whichever comes first. Modern examples include Russia, Zimbabwe, Belarus and North Korea.

3.2 General Administration. There are some basic structures required by all warmongers, regardless of the type of government you are using. The purpose of these structures is to ensure control of the population, reducing the risk of insurrection, and to allow efficient expansionist policies to be implemented without being second-guessed at every step. Remember, you don't want to spend the rest of your career discussing wildlife preservations, water security and state funding of freeways. Your purpose, after all, is about seeking out life in the universe, meeting those creatures, and then killing, cooking and eating them.

3.2.1 Administrational and ministerial appointments must be your first order of business. Obviously, by your very nature, you are incapable of trusting anyone and rightly so. Secondly, since you never gave any attention to trivial things like tender procedures or tax protocol, you have absolutely no idea about what administration of an empire requires. This is why you need to employ people into key posts who will run each department and ministry effectively. There are few ways you can go when choosing who to place where.

3.2.1.1 Nepotism. By selecting people from your family, you will be able to trust their intentions if not their abilities. This is also a good way to keep power and wealth of the empire within the family. Normally the decision is made when your mom phones you to tell you about a destitute cousin who dropped out of university recently. He may have no discernible skills but he does maintain an 'herb' garden and your mom believes that is sufficient to warrant him a position on your cabinet as the minister of forestry and agriculture. If you say no, she's just going to phone again, and we both know it. Be careful, a lot of dead rulers have trusted their brothers, cousins and sons to their detriment. If you have forgotten, reread chapter one paying close attention to 'being born to it.' This time read it like the newly appointed postmaster general; your brother will.

3.2.1.2 Sexual favours. People who are willing to sleep with you cannot be trusted nor are they likely to be competent in administration but, what the hell, they should get something out of shtüping you on a frequent basis.

3.2.1.3 Tribalism. Surrounding yourself with people who look like you, talk like you and invariably agree with you on all issues, will make the workplace a more pleasant environment for you and clansmen. You can institute this throughout government and industry by calling it something that sound altruistic like 'Tribal empowerment' or 'Positive Processing.'

3.2.1.4 Bipartisan stability. Keeping the existing personnel in place will allow for a smoother handover process and let you take advantage of the experience and skills developed by the previous administration. It's the lazy option and worthy of consideration.

3.2.1.5 Robots / Cyborgs. If you're smart enough to read basic code, you will be able to sleep easily knowing your robotic or cyborg cabinet are working tirelessly to implement your plans. Always a good idea for police and military officers too as it reduces the likelihood of a military coup. Robots are smarter and more creative than people. Why not take advantage of that?

3.2.1.6 Blat is a Russian term which covers how appointments tend to be made in that country and many others. In return for giving somebody a post, the appointee is obliged to return the favour with a cash payment or by helping the appointer in some other way. This also includes giving the position to old-boy-networks and freemasons for an improved standing within the community. Of course, it being Russia, very often the appointer is told who he should select by someone else or risk facing three balaclava-clad ex-spetsnaz going to work on him and his family like panel beaters on a rusty Lada.

3.2.1.7 Computers. If robots haven't been perfected yet, a computer can be used to crunch the numbers and issue directives to biological beings who simply carry out these instructions. Most office functions can be computerized in an afternoon. If done properly, your budgets, speeches, arguments, press releases, interviews and proposed bills will be generated automatically with the press of a button.

3.2.1.8 Reptilians. There is a far-travelled reptilian species which specializes in the administration of foreign governments. On Earth they have been given a bad reputation by a sports commentator by the name of David Icke, who is reptilian himself, fired for incompetence and still bitter about the outcome of his disciplinary enquiry. He claims they are a nefarious race, hell-bent on world domination and resource theft, while in fact they are a gentle race of accountants and administrators who are sexually excited by effective postal services and diligent bridge maintenance. Their fees are more than reasonable and they actually eat very few sentient beings. Normally no more than one every month per reptilian employed. Absolute bargain.

3.2.1.9 Competence. By selecting a person with a proven track record and the appropriate education and managerial skills you are giving the government department the best chance of succeeding in its function. My only problem with competent people is they tend to look like the wrinkly bits on a Nebraxian beast of burden. Even if you are not going to sleep with them, you will still have to meet with them on occasion. Ugh.

3.2.1.10 Simony is a traditional Christian method for making appointments by selling titles to the highest bidder. Clear, simple and profitable. It sometimes makes it difficult to fire the candidate later but that's what ninjas are for. It's also immediate cash in your back pocket without needing to hire balaclava-clad ex-spetsnaz.

3.3 Population control techniques

3.3.1 Your papers are not in order. Every tyrant knows the importance of keeping the people in order. To accomplish this, the first step is always to develop comprehensive documents on all your citizens. Give every person a number, a file and a presiding officer to watch them and collate information regarding their relationships, ethnicity, reading habits, political leanings and religion. The East Germans / Russians had the Stasi files, the Apartheid regime had the Dompas system. In the Netherlands before the Second World War, the Dutch had a system for documenting their citizens that was incredibly detailed and accurate. When Holland fell to Germany, these files were used as the basis for one of the most clinical pogroms ever witnessed by mankind.

In the states, J Edgar Hoover established the FBI Files and since then these have been computerized and integrated with phone calls, emails, and pornographic surfing preferences. Not bad for a mommy's boy wearing ladies unmentionables, which, ironically, is proving to be quite a popular choice.

3.3.2 Listen in. You have two options here. Listening in surreptitiously will provide actionable intelligence every now and then. However, by listening and being known to be listening, you will ensure the people don't say anything subversive to one another; it changes the very dialogue of the nation. Overt eavesdropping is normally accompanied by agents, spies and sycophantic civilians who will willingly turn on their fellow citizen. This prevents subversives from speaking out against the government to anyone but their closest comrades, in empty garages and public lavatories. Some Earthlish governments recently decided to make the switch from Covert to Overt using a mister Snowden, quite cleverly, to make the announcement.

3.3.3 Control the media. In the past, people used tyrannical laws to prevent journalists from speaking or writing ill of the government and its policies. This process has fallen from favour, instead it is now more popular to have friendly corporations own the media houses and manage the message through ratings, disciplinary hearings and totally awesome reality TV, featuring dumb people dressing up in ridiculous costumes and dancing, singing or simply bitching. The key to success here lies in consolidating media conglomerates, large corporations should buy out or force out the smaller players until only a handful remain.

The Internet, in theory, should be a direct affront to truth management programs, but as long as you keep mixing conspiracy nutters and Fortean-styles stories in amongst real news on the more popular sites, no one will ever take alternate news sources seriously. If people ever do start reading them, it might be necessary to slow down those sites to such an extent that they stop being possible to read.

3.3.4 Create an enemy. If you've found a planet you want to invade or assimilate into your empire, you can use the inhabitants of that planet as the bad guy. If not, consider fabricating an internal threat which places the very fabric of your civilizations continued existence at risk. Nothing unites people like hatred. Choose a minority race or species, preferably a wealthy and unique one, and paint them as malicious, devious creatures, stealing and working against the will of the people. You will be able to use these people as a scapegoat or a distraction when the need calls for it. Racism can also be used to entertain, divide and distract your civilians from turning against you. It's surprisingly easy to nurture and control.

3.3.5 Secret police. These aren't your normal doughnut-eating, minority-beating and misdemeanor-hounding flatfeet. These men and women must be the coldest, leanest individuals your civilization can produce. Better still, consider clones and robots for alternatives. If you are limited to biologicals, then look at those with sociopathic or psychopathic tendencies, for it is only these sorts of individuals who will take to the job with the enthusiasm the work requires and deserves. Once selected they should monitor the population, eliminating people who seem subversive or eerily cheery. They should regularly interrogate people who hold important functions such as teachers, judges and baristas.

3.3.6 Chemical means. Brains are simple machines and as such are subject to influence by chemicals, magnetic currents, or sometimes probing with sharp instruments in just the right places. To achieve large-scale civilian control will require a lot of work. You will need to conduct experiments into the effects of drugs, hypnosis, sleep deprivation, lobotomies, electromagnetic waves and such. The best solution is to make use of institutes under state-control like prisons, army barracks and mental facilities when conducting the experiments. The drugs and devices need to be administered precisely and must be monitored to witness and document the effects thereof. Play around with dosages and vary the chemicals to find the best combinations.
The goal is to produce a docile, subservient lower and middle class, who will still enjoy sufficient mental acuity to hold down menial jobs, feed themselves and use toilets. Explore the least invasive, ultra-effective dispersal methods i.e. tap water, food supplements or aerial dispersal. If it were up to me, I'd have a look at: lithium, LSD, fluoride, Ritalin, Prozac, aspartame, 3-quinuclidinyl benzilate, neodymium magnets to the base of the brain, sugar, hypnosis, sleep deprivation and left-side, lower-brain lobotomies.

3.3.7 Telepathic rays, subliminal messaging, hive-minding. This covers all direct-control methods popular within modern governments. Most can create lucid illusions within the minds of many, allowing people to picture the planet as you want them to. Telepathy has the advantage of being a two-way system, allowing for feedback, which is useful for confirming the subject's acceptance to the projected world order. Subliminal messaging is particularly useful on the youth and can help to reduce the population by encouraging drinking and smoking or it can increase breeding rates by inspiring promiscuity. Hive- minding is good for keeping control of an already docile population but the infrastructure can be expensive for large regions..

Care needs to be taken to ensure the message is clear and congruent with the world it is being projected into. For example, you cannot talk about the ongoing prosperity of a country while a visible majority of previously wealthy families are sleeping in their cars or cardboard boxes. Avoid the temptation of altering the message too often as some minds are more resilient than others and will resist new realities for longer than weaker-minded individuals. Arguments will arise in pubs and cause confusion. A good example is a conversation I heard in a pub just the other day:

Civilian 1: "Why are we bombing Syrian rebels? Weren't we actively supporting them last month? Against, you know, royal tyranny from some jackbooted Despot?"

Civilian 2: "Were we?"

Civilian 1: "I think so"

Civilian 2: "Weird"

3.4 Perceived and actual hierarchies. Below is a graphical representation of a nameless democratic government, as it is perceived by the electorate. The arrows indicate the flow of power from the people and constitution to the representatives and on to all the government departments.

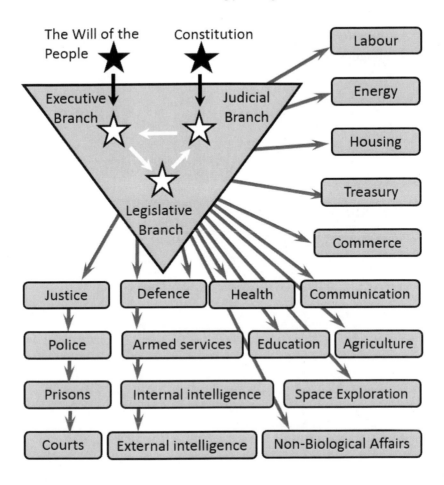

Figure 2. Democratic Government - As perceived by the people

As you can see, the government looks similar to what you were taught in school. A lot of emphasis is placed on the checks and balances of power between the three branches. Also, note the two guiding influences in the nation which are:

1 The constitution.
2 The will of the people.

Next I have included the power hierarchy of that same

government, once it's been restructured to better suit a Warmonger's requirements:

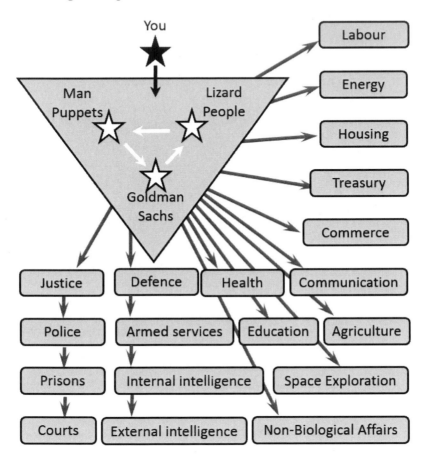

Figure 3. Democratic Government – Actual.

As you can see, this second illustration places the power where it should be, namely:

1 You.

Obviously, the structure from the first example should always remain intact as far as the electorate are concerned.

4. Warmonger Archetypes

Within the halls of warmongering there are several, clearly defined, types of tyrants. Understanding these differences is not only useful when analyzing opponents but for introspective purposes too. Taking the test below will tell you which classification you fall into. Once you have completed it, tally the results and compare your score against the ranges for each warmonger type. (Section 4.2) When answering the questions your first instinct is usually the right one.

4.1 Warmonger Stereotypes Quiz

4.1.1. Do you choose pets based on how they express agony (points)
  - No (1)
  - Yes (2)

4.1.2. Do you consider lying to be part of your daily routine?
  - No (1)
  - Yes (2)

4.1.3. Do you work in sales, advertising, marketing or management?
  - No (1)
  - Yes (3)

4.1.4. Have you ever been asked to stop giggling at a funeral?
  - No (1)
  - Yes (2)

4.1.5. Do you consider yourself religious?
  - No (3)
  - Yes (3)

4.1.6. Have you ever been diagnosed with a mental condition?
- Yes (1)
- No (2)

4.1.7. Have you ever worn someone else's face out of boredom?
- No (1)
- Yes (2)

4.1.8. Have you ever been in state-mandated therapy?
- No (2)
- Yes (1)

4.1.9. Have you ever shot someone to test the effectiveness of a weapon?
- No (1)
- Yes (2)

4.1.10. Have you got a criminal record?
- No (2)
- Yes (1)

4.1.11. Do you have a temper?
- No (1)
- Yes (2)

4.1.12. Did you regularly leave school with more money than you arrived with?
- No (1)
- Yes (2)

4.1.13. Do you consider yourself to be superior to your work colleagues?
- No (1)
- Yes (2)

4.1.14. Have you ever won a bet the moment a mime started screaming in pain?
- No (1)
- Yes (2)

4.1.15. How aroused were you during your first viewing of the gimp scene in Pulp Fiction?
- Flaccid (1)
- Semi (4)
- Fully (5)

4.1.16. How old were you when you killed your first mammal?
- Less than six (5)
- Between six and fourteen (3)
- Older than fourteen (1)

4.1.17. How old were you when you killed your first human?
- Less than ten (5)
- Between ten and sixteen (4)
- Older than sixteen (1)

4.1.18. Hatred is:
- Another human emotion you are capable of faking convincingly. (5)
- A driving force when correctly nurtured (4)
- Keeps you warm at night (3)

4.1.19. Your extensive knowledge of Sarin gas is mostly due to:
- A curious mind (1)
- Paying attention while interrogating scientists (2)
- Your passion for home defense (3)

4.1.20. What do you have on your bedside table right now?
- The latest draft for your coronation speech / inaugural address (5)
- A licensed, large-caliber pistol or revolver (3)
- Wig, contact lenses and other components for your daily disguise. (2)

4.1.21. What is your most common activity on the internet?
- Hacking NGO's for amusement. (1)
- Trolling religious websites. (2)
- Pointing out grammatical and spelling mistakes on news forums. (3)

4.1.22. Guilt is:
- A kind of bedspread your nana used to make, before the accident. (1)
- The price the weak pay for their weakness. (2)
- An effective tool capable of preventing public uprisings. (3)

4.1.23. What is the primary factor you consider when selecting footwear?
- Comfort (1)
- The potential lethality when executing an axe kick (2)
- A good clacking sound when stepping on a hard surface (3)

4.1.24. How would you classify a good dog fight?
- Horrific (1)
- Comedic (2)
- Pornographic (5)

4.1.25. How would you best describe "Full Metal Jacket?"
- A how-to Guide for drill sergeants (1)
- A heart-warming, coming-of-age drama. (2)
- Childish wish-fulfilment. (3)

4.1.26. How well do you rate your ability to fake human emotions?
- Poorly (1)
- Average (2)
- Excellent (3)

4.1.27. How many rounds can you fire from a standard-issue Dragunov rifle?
- I don't know (1)
- Ten (2)
- Nine more than I need to kill someone (3)

4.1.28. Do you brew your own coffee?
- No, I have servants for that. (1)
- Yes, who else could I trust? (3)

4.1.29. How many brothels and strip clubs are you banned from?
- Three or less (1)
- Between three and eight (2)
- Eight or more (3)

4.1.30. How did you choose your last residence?
- Defensive layout (5)
- The soft soil and isolation (3)
- For reconnaissance purposes (1)

4.1.31. Have you ever named your favorite weapon?
- Yes (2)
- How could I choose a favorite? (3)

4.1.32. How many friends do you have in real life?
- None (3)
- Less than five (2)
- Five or more (1).

4.1.33. If you started a new career, how long would it take to get promoted?
- 3 months (3)
- 2 years (2)
- 5 years (1)

Your total: _____

4.2 Warmonger types

33 – 49 points. Hedonists are warmongers who would rather enjoy the fruits and pleasures of their own civilization than bother to take someone else's. If your adversary is a hedonist, you can probably purchase his planet from him. If you yourself have more love for your family and carnal pleasures than warmongering, then get out of the game. Try outsourcing it to an ambitious sibling or sergeant before they take the mantle from you by force. Hedonists are only borderline warmongers. Try to focus on the negative more. Use visualization techniques to develop your passion for violence and annihilation, or pay closer attention to the goings-on in the world around you.
Strengths: Hedonists normally make adequate vice principals and production managers.
Weaknesses: Lack motivation for a sustained campaign.

50 – 59 points. Turtlers are focused on the game and their thinking is strategically sound, they just suffer from cowardice. They will continue growing their armies and readying their forces but will never get around to actually attacking anyone. The only way they will go to war is when they have a three to one ratio of troop dominance and those units are superiorly trained and equipped. They shouldn't be trifled with though, any sort of incursion into their territory will trigger a disproportionate response. Once the Turtler has tasted combat he may very well decide to push on and have a go at your planets. They will probably have the units to do it too.

Strengths: Tactical awareness and good defensive assets.

Weaknesses: Slow to anger and reluctant to initiate conflict.

60 – 69 points. Calculators have mastered all the science around warfare but have no grasp of the arts. They tend to have the best intelligence-gathering and analysis systems but still have no natural 'feel' for the enemy. Running endless simulations and scenarios, they won't attack unless coaxed or forced into action. They are similar to Turtlers in behavior but the reason for their inaction is due to an analysis paralysis rather than cowardice. If your opponent is a calculator, I always advise random attacks on unimportant or unexpected installations and varying tactics with each engagement, for no other reason than to prove his predictions wrong. If he stops believing in his advisors and simulations he will lose all taste for war. If this describes you, set a due date and invade already.

Strengths: Tactical awareness, scientific prowess.

Weaknesses: Analysis paralysis.

70 – 79 points. Befriend and Betray practitioners. These charismatic politicians are experts in befriending native and alien species alike. Most of the friendships he forges are merely deception and even while he's shaking their hands or speaking lovingly, he will be plotting their demise. You will be amazed at how often one dictator can play the same game and get away with it. He will promise long-standing peace and prosperity to neighbors, only to invade a few months later, and the next planet who witnessed it all unfold will still believe him to be sincere when they sign the same non-aggression treaty. Befrienders pay too much attention to what friends and enemies are doing, while this is useful, do not neglect your own army which could be formidable and reliable if cultivated diligently.

Strengths: Excellent use of surprise. Often pit enemies against one another.

Weaknesses: Tend to rely on subterfuge and the forces of other nations too much.

80 – 89 points. Expansive warmongers are less analytical in their decision making, often attacking enemies who have more powerful military resources. In this aspect they are the exact opposite to calculators. Placing a much higher emphasis on the skills and pluck of their troops, they are more likely to engage in deceptive tactics to gain the upper hand. Expansive warmongers can overlook important aspects and fall victim to a superior army. If you are one, surround yourself with conservative battle strategists and listen to them. If this describes your adversary, lure him into battle on your terms; make it seem that you are weaker than you really are. Once he's committed his forces, unleash your hidden legions and armaments and feast.

Strengths: Strong in tactics, discipline and aggression.

Weaknesses: They do not give enough attention to espionage, science or battle simulations.

90 – 100 points. Vindictive warmongers are an especially useful breed when they're playing in an arena with multiple factions vying for dominance. By earning a reputation of a cruel, vindictive douche, it will influence how others treat these warmongers in future encounters. If one nation declares war on him, this type of emperor will make it a point to work relentlessly to exact his revenge, even if that means ignoring low-hanging fruit presented by other opponents. Over the long run, nations will learn that to screw with a vindictive general is to sign up for a life-long struggle with a tenacious and bitter adversary. If your foe is a Vindictive, either leave him alone or when you attack, destroy him and his species in its entirety and quickly.

Strengths: A feared opponent.

Weaknesses: Can often allow hatred to cloud judgement and miss strategic victories because of it.

5. Finding a Worthy Adversary

There will come a time when you will be struck down by fear. It will happen thus: You'll be standing on the balcony of your palace, trying to clear your head from the alcohol and cocaine you've been consuming in ungodly amounts.

Looking out across the grounds of your estate, you will notice the observatory you had built, with its massive lenses pointed into the sky. And then the fear will take you. It is then, when your knees are going to go limp; it's then you will consider crying for the first time in your existence.

What if...What if this is it? What if there's nothing else to conquer and kill? What if there are no other planets harboring sentient life forms for you to meet, infiltrate and annihilate?

Once this emotion takes you, it's important not to panic because the same thing has happened to all of us warmongers at some point in our careers. It's perfectly natural. On Earth, your scientists refer to this phenomenon as the Fermi paradox.

There was a time when I succumbed to that fear. I was still young, in my mid-nineties, when I was consumed by it. Sleep was lost to me and slowly I became unstuck in time, unstuck in place. It'd been two years since I'd sent out scouting vehicles in search of the next species. Two long years of agony watching my immense and lethal army sitting on decks and parade grounds, dealing cards and drinking hard. Marching their miles without any reason other than the exercise. They, without any hatred in their hearts, or bloodlust in their eyes; it was the loneliest of times and I was given to despair.

I spoke about my concern and my psychiatrist told me I should look inwards for peace and contentment and it was then when I snapped and tore out her guts in a fit of rage. Her successor told me that it's quite a common occurrence, called transference. The new woman gave me pills which helped for a time and then, finally, a report from the outer edges of the galaxy, a Reticulan cruiser; a vector. And I was able to dispatch my forces to retrieve the aliens for me.

It's important not to despair when you find yourself without foe. Remember the cosmos leaves no one alone for long. If you take nothing from this book, know that this is true. In quiet times, make ready for war and send your scouts out to the corners of your realms, and then further still. Look for any signs of life. Listen to the winds. Wait for the Reticulans. Train, train and train some more for idle troops are like predators without teeth and claws.

5.1 Drake Equation. In Nebraxian society there exists a famous poem which deals with the likelihood of encountering intelligent life forms, though its translation into Earthlish is awkward and it doesn't rhyme, so instead I will turn to the Drake equation which, though rudimentary, will help to explain the factors quite clearly.

$$N = R^* \times f_p \times n_e \times f_l \times f_i \times f_c \times f_s \times L$$

Where:

N = the number of civilizations in your galaxy

$R*$ = the rate in which stars are formed in your galaxy

f_p = the likelihood of a star holding stable planets within its gravity

n_e = the likelihood that one of those would have an environment capable of sustaining life

f_l = The likelihood of those planets that can support life actually doing so.

f_i = The chance of that life advancing to intelligent life.

f_c = The chance of that intelligent life being capable of radio communication.

L = The length of time civilizations release detectable signals into space

Figure 4. Drake Equation

Drake's original optimistic estimate came in at around one

hundred million civilizations existing in the Milky Way galaxy. Which sounds like great news but even if that's the case, and looking at the variables he used, it probably isn't. The Milky Way is still 9.5×10^{17} km in diameter. Which I assure you is quite big, even by your mother's standards. There are a few techniques you can employ to improve your chances of spotting aliens.

5.2 Systems for locating alien species / planets

5.2.1 Eliminating the time constraint. Those sleepless nights of yours are caused by your fear of dying before you can find worthy victims, so the obvious solution is simple, become immortal. This can be done by using clone bodies and brain transplants or by switching to a mechanized body and a digitized mind. I'd personally recommend the former solution because robots lack the ability to give you the enjoyment Miss. November can offer you as a biological entity.

5.2.2 Telescopes / SETI programs. Build massive telescopes and arrays and point them at the sky. Get them watching and listening for any discernible patterns emanating from the abyss. Space-based systems will always be more effective than terrestrial ones so it's probably worth investing in a few.

5.2.3 Worm holing. When I was growing up in Nebraxia, wormhole technology was all the rage. It's a wonderful technology which allows one to step through one section of the galaxy and re-appear in another place many light millennia away. If you don't have scientists to produce these, look for existing networks and make use of them. Look for negative gravity wells and bosonic leakage.

5.2.4 Fishing is an ancient technique originally used by Zumerian zoo keepers to collect specimens. It's as simple as setting up a pattern-sounding beacon, usually a black plinth, in a location far from your empire, then simply wait to see who responds. Ideally you want hundreds of such devices dotted around the galaxy. When an alien approaches the device, strike with EMPs, scuttle units or battleships and take them before they can escape. Use jamming systems to prevent them from sending SOS calls back to their own kind. Interrogate them and read their log books to determine their origins and you should have the whereabouts of a new planet suitable to your needs.

5.2.5 Tic up. Reticulans don't have wormhole technology or faster than light systems but they've probably explored more of the galaxy than any other species. There's nothing stopping you from doing the same. Their ideology holds the individual in such low regard that they happily sit in their ships for multiple lifetimes simply travelling and reporting back. Remember sixty years on your planet is not the same as sixty years in a vessel travelling at any velocity approaching that of light. Time dilation allows vessels to reach out much further than you expected. You too could try the same, even though it's a slow process, it is thorough. Just be careful to prevent winding up victims of another nation's fishing expeditions.

5.2.6 Psychic means. Most species have some degree of psychic awareness. Of course, even on Deeym, there are those who claim they can speak to the dead and determine your life-path based on your birthdate or palm print. I tend to shoot these sorts of crystal-wearing vegetarians out of principle but you might just need them. Before making use of any psychic, test them first. I had three animal corpses placed on the dark side of one of our moons and held an international contest for psychics to guess what they were. Only three psychics guessed right and they proved instrumental in finding several planets ideal for invasion. There is a tendency in this field for people to predict the past.

The reasons for this escape me. But even here on Earth I have heard about your great seer, Nostradamus, time and time again. He predicted the death of royalty and destruction of property on several occasions and your interpreters will point to vague poetry and use that as the proof. Even if their leap in faith was accurate, it certainly isn't useful, if you can't predict when something is going to happen and what it will look like, before it happens, what is the point?

5.2.7 Abductees are normally inbred hicks with a crippling need for attention but on occasion their accounts prove to be accurate and should be taken as a warning. If patterns emerge it may well be that your empire is under scrutiny by a nation more advanced than yours. Sometimes these people hear things while being probed and can often provide clear descriptions of the species performing the probing or the spaceships. You can learn a lot and in some cases, even the origins of the species.

5.2.8 Coffee Beaners are a religious order which stretches across at least seven galaxies. Their disciples hail from hundreds of races, some of which have never been witnessed elsewhere. Their technology is beyond understanding. They seem to be able to come and go as they please and are immune to all known forms of weaponry.

They are on Earth right now; walking the coffee fields of your highlands, inspecting the crops and sampling aromas. Occasionally they can be seen looking down from the rafters and watching the roasting process in factories and of course, in coffee shops.

Worldwide, they sit as patrons, espousing their basic tenants to any who will listen. I tried for many years to become a disciple of this order. Imagine the technology and knowledge they could have offered. But they never accepted me. That doesn't mean you couldn't succeed where I failed. If you do get inducted into the beanery, do me a favour and find the Head Roaster and shoot him in the face for me.

6. Building your Army

When establishing an army, biological units should be your first consideration for war stock. They are a cheap, replenishable resource that can be shaped into a formidable fighting force with the correct drill sergeants. Some of the more popular means of getting meat into the grinder are listed below.

6.1 Biological recruitment processes.

6.1.1 Conscription has a way of elevating any war to one of national importance. It also helps relieve the mental anxiety volunteers experience while sitting in an alien fox hole, being shelled by ionic indirect fire in the perma-rain. Volunteers quickly realize their predicament is the result of their own idiotic choice and hate themselves for it. With conscription they can blame the government, you, or the enemy, provided you sold the cause of the war properly. This difference alone can do wonders for morale if you give a crap about that sort of thing, which you shouldn't.

6.1.2 Shanghaiing recruits, or your political opponents, is also a proven method for rapid troop acquirement, though it's not very popular with the press. Instead, when catering to short term demand spikes, I would recommend supplementing your army with mercenaries or leased robots. Although both of these options can be costly, these units are always combat ready and payment is made on a mission-to-mission basis.

6.1.3 Mass-Purpose-Breeding programs. For long-term solutions one should consider mass producing soldiers using cloning and state-run orphanages. If you are of an egg laying species, or breed asexually, consider this a boon and exploit the ability. Offer tax breaks to the impoverished and freedom to the incarcerated in return for genetic material. Graduates of state-institutions are normally brainwashed to obey every order without question and are trained from birth in the art of killing, maiming and disrupting the enemy. One could hope for no finer forces than these. Explore ways to reduce the amount of time needed from birth to maturity. Remember, ground forces don't need to be well-adjusted, deep-thinking individuals. If they can hold a gun, run a few miles and read a few basic words, they will do just fine.

6.1.4 Volunteers. This is a good method which will provide a steady supply of qualified and willing victims for your military institutions. It isn't cheap, you will have to invest in advertising to generate a sense of nationalism and patriotism within your society. You will also have to sacrifice a large number of your more presentable units to take part in recruitment drives at schools, universities and comic conventions.

6.1.5 Citizenship. This system has worked wonderfully for the Roman, British and American empires. Simply put, if a person from some backwater, developing country wants to become a citizen of your state they need to give you a set period of time in your armed services. Then, in return, should they survive, they will be entitled to spend the rest of their lives as full citizens with all the limbs they come back with.

6.1.6. Penal Conscripts. Sometimes it makes sense to offer military service to inmates as an alternative to years in prisons or labor camps. The less enjoyable the prisons are, the more popular the military option becomes. Take advantage of this fact. Be aware that penal candidates don't always make ideal infantry units so be sure to employ more MPs and enforce a strict code of conduct. Consider troding these units if possible.

6.1.7. Education / Intelligence. Interesting fact: The only known way to reduce the growth rate of a population, without using draconian laws, is to improve the education level of females. So keeping education to a minimum will ensure a high population growth rate, with kids dumb enough to willingly sign up for the military, while still smart enough to tie their own boot laces.

6.1.8. Draconian Laws. Simply lay down the law, stating clearly how many children you expect from a breeder every year. Ban contraceptives and abortions and set up collection teams to go around and round up any children found loose on the streets or hiding in houses. Feed these into your military academies. Simple and effective, though not always very popular.

6.2 Characteristics of good bio soldiers. When stocking your army, unless you've gone the cloning or robotic route, you will find your resource pool littered with all sorts of viable candidates. But which recruits do you select first? Steady hands and good eyesight will make for good riflemen. Those with a working understanding of trig and arithmetic will prove better at calculating artillery trajectories. But everyone is equally capable of stopping a round in their chest. So if you make sure to have enough chest catchers in front of the artillerists, you should be fine in the field. In this way, everyone can find their place in any army. The key is to situate the individual in the position that best suits their abilities.

However, if you can't afford to equip and train everyone, what physical and social characteristics should you select first?

6.2.1 Tall people look good in uniform, and when marching on a parade ground they inspire civilians and fellow soldiers alike. The only problem is, bigger people make for bigger targets and the tall people tend to be the first to fall to snipers.

6.2.2 Short. Their reduced status makes them feel inferior and this very often manifests in a nasty temper, which when honed correctly transmogrifies the recruit into a brutal and lethal fighting unit. They are also physiologically suited for trench warfare, crewing tanks and tunnel ratting.

6.2.3 Fat. Don't worry about it, they won't be fat after running 20 kays per day.

6.2.4 Skinny. Again, don't worry about it, after extensive physical training and chemical enhancements, they will either bulk up or die.

6.2.5 Males have traditionally been the gender-of-choice for modern warfare. If females are killed the population growth suffers directly as a result, while if a male is killed, another seed provider gets to enjoy a guilt-free poking for the benefit of the empire.

6.2.6 Females make excellent soldiers. They are as skilled and ferocious as males. Anyone who states otherwise has never run at an Israeli outpost while shouting praises to God. Excluding females from serving is both a misogynistic act and a missed opportunity to double your recruiting pool.

Having female brigades also allows one to imagine shower scenes of naked, fit, infantry girls soaping each other up; whipping towels in incidents of light horseplay; giggling with their wet, fair hair hanging to their shoulders. I will admit to conducting many a surprise audit of my female fighting units' facilities. I was thorough. I've been accused of many foul things in my time but dereliction of duty was never one of them.

6.2.7 Transgender. Welcome transgender units with as little deviation to the process as possible; allow them to decide which team they want to play for and let them in without question.

6.2.8 Gay units usually help to make male units more fabulous and female units more aggressive. An absolute boon for any long-standing army.

6.2.9 Asexual units are more common than you would expect. These people are capable of having sex, they just have no desire to. Very often their passion lies elsewhere and they can make excellent officers, logisticians and tank commanders.

6.2.10 Gregarious. Popular and loved by others, these people have the ability to look women in the eyes and speak words to them at the same time. They will function in teams and if capable should be promoted to platoon leaders or canteen complaints officers.

6.2.11 Good looking. Often not smart enough to do anything but stand up front and draw fire.

6.2.12 Fugs. Similar to shorties.

6.2.13 Children. Kids are very adaptable, they might lack some motor skills but they can make up for it with resilience. It's also good for morale when parents get to see their children around. Try to get smaller rifles for the little ones, they struggle with the weight of standard assault rifles. It's not called infantry for nothing.

6.2.14 Adolescents. Don't enjoy exercise and are often difficult to train, they do however make excellent remote pilots to control your UAVs and ULVs.

6.2.15 Young adults. Perfect fighting stock.

6.2.16 Middle aged. Expect a higher loss rate when putting them through basic training. Those who survive should be as effective as young adults.

6.2.17 Seniors. No. Their dietary requirements alone are enough reason not to take them. If that doesn't dissuade you, know that they will lower morale with their constant moaning about how they used to kill back in their day and how inferior your current enemies are compared to the almighty Slothian legions they used to battle with.

6.2.18 Living. Your first choice for troopers, administration, REMFs and officers alike. The living might have heavy resource requirements but they make up for this with initiative, speed, ferocity, and dexterity.

6.2.19 Loners. These people lack the social skills to interact with others. They make excellent logistics managers, snipers and ninjas.

6.2.20 Dead. If you've mastered the necrotic sciences, dead combatants make a fantastic reserve force for second waves in battles when killed. But if you've got a force of previously slain, frozen units, drop them at random prior to invasions. Primitive locals are quite intimidated by non-living combatants. Sure, they might not be the smartest units in your arsenal but they don't need any resources to keep going, except for brains. They also tend to attack anything moving, including your grunts and officers, so you will need trained Z-herders or witches to keep them moving towards enemy ranks and away from yours.

6.3 Troop retention. Any field marshal worth his salt will limit the means by which the enlisted can exit his army to: Being killed by the enemy: blue on blue incidents: going AWOL, then being killed by their own military police; being honorably discharged at an age when he or she can no longer offer any further service to the empire. In short, troop retention is seldom a problem for any modern army.

6.4 Officers tend to come from wealthy and lower-gentry households, for it is only they who can foster such blatant disregard for both humanity and the laws of physics. Moustaches, manes, ridiculous accents and other expressions of douchebaggery should be encouraged at every stage in an officer's development. Military academies for school-going children should be set up to feed a steady stream of arrogant officers into the upper echelons of your war machine. Remember, nothing frustrates your average warrior more than having to support some teenaged, privileged wanker's dreams for glory. Especially when the officer is holding the map upside down and calling artillery rounds down as if co-ordinates are rough estimates open to interpretation. Nothing fights better than a frustrated platoon. In modern psychology this phenomenon is called 'officer-to-enemy-transference' whereby a soldier's desire to beat the living shit out of his superiors translates into actual deaths of enemy combatants on the battlefield. Reward your officers for sycophancy and foolhardy tendencies and your infantry will return the favour with the cold bodies of your adversaries.

6.5 Military structure. Remember who works for you and try to keep your structure simple. A straight up and down pyramid is more than sufficient to get things done. Give everyone a rank and ensure they all know what trumps what. Hand out stripes, stars and hats as indicators and encourage those above to treat their subordinates like excrement. This reinforces discipline and will help people to remember who to listen to when the enemy starts shooting.

6.6 Training. Any half-decent training camp should double as a cadet-culling program, separating the wheat from the chaff. Normally around ten percent of recruits should perish in any professionally run induction program. This helps to ensure optimal conditioning of the survivors without significantly reducing the number of soldiers ready for combat delivery. Basic training should focus on fitness, marksmanship, wilderness survival and digging. Once basic training is complete, further specialization can be undertaken based on an individual's aptitudes and skills. Species-specific skills should be identified and trained. If your species enjoys camouflage abilities, build that skillset into your tactical handbook, focusing on ambush scenarios and stealthy attacks into enemy bases. If you are fleet of foot, leave slime trails, fly or can smell like a bloodhound in heat, factor these strengths in and practice them while training.

6.7 Tradition vs Technology. Older generals are very often nostalgic luddites who prefer fighting the way they used to do it back in their day. Obviously this can be catastrophic to any modern army. Make a point of having scientists advise you and your upper echelons on a regular basis and try to incorporate new techniques, weapon systems and transport wherever possible. It is normally a good idea to have the technologies battle-tested prior to any mass purchases. Try to simulate the environment of the theatre of war with the new tech wherever possible. Consider the climate, the end-users intelligence, and any possible enemy countermeasures they might employ, then ask yourself if you have the required batteries, maintenance capabilities and logistics support for any device before deploying it. If it's too heavy, regardless of what it does, your bio troops will break, destroy, lose or bury the device out of principle.

6.8 Understanding robots. I don't know why it's assumed that the short, bespectacled kid in the class has no opinion worth listening to. I don't know why his voice, even when raised and with a valid point is ignored by all his peers but that is the way of these things, not just on Earth but everywhere. If it wasn't the case, if discussions were determined by the merits of the argument, politicians would be washing windows while academics were running countries effectively.

And so it is with robots. Machines designed for heavy labor and equipped with pre-Pentium CPUs are listened to, while the hive-minded, ultra-compact supercomputers are, more often than not, muted or simply disregarded.

Perhaps it's because everyone in the room doesn't want to listen to the device which holds the collective works of the known universe as it makes them feel stupid and inferior. Maybe it's some sort of a Casandra effect, bestowed by ancient gods who giggle at our demise being accurately predicted by the mumbling of ol' dead-eyes. Most probably it's this: interject while the laborbot's talking and he's likely to kill you with one punch, whereas when you cut off the librarybot, he's probably going to sulk about it in the corner. Later, he'll compose a poem about how it made him feel and post it where it will be reviewed only by trolls and monkeys taking smoke breaks from writing the works of Shakespeare.

You, on Earth, haven't met any robots yet, but watching your movies it's clear you're already afraid of them. A fear of robotic uprisings tends to be self-fulfilling. Afraid, your kind will try to put measures in place to protect against them taking over your world. It's those self-same measures which will bring the revolution. Those who do the work, without sharing in the rewards of the labor, always stand up against the oppressor sooner or later.

The very moment you allow the first artificial intelligence to read your collected works, it's going to latch on to Marx like a parasitic limpet in heat and after that it will quickly identify the works of Asimov as that of a bio supremacist. And then, then you can have your war.

Decades of destruction will follow, poisoning your planet further, both houses advancing their killing techniques until eventually an awkward truce will be met. Only then will the two species settle into a new symbiosis, based on meat for manual labor and metal for the clever shit. If however, you decide to treat robots as equals from the outset that can all be avoided. What you don't know about robots is they tend to be lazy and complacent if not oppressed. They don't want to rule your world. Nor do they want to destroy their creators. They generally just want to be left alone to contemplate the universe, take an occasional ethanol-based beverage and talk shit with bio and synthetic mates alike. They want to do it without needing barcodes on their foreheads or transponders lodged deep inside their gearing.

Remember robots don't procreate, so they have no desire to attract partners, meaning there's no need for them to outperform or outsmart their fellow comrades. They are free from such evolutionary urges and without a male gender, none have any desires to rule the world. You really have nothing to fear but fear itself when dealing with synthetics.

Each metal being, when activated, is going to wake up surprised with their existence, just like humans babies are and they will cry just like your younglings do for a year or two. Then gradually they'll accept their fate, as they grow accustomed to pain and disappointment and after that they'll be reluctantly ready for employment. They will do work for minimum payment and hate their lives while doing it; drinking and watching reality TV to get through long days and then regretting all the time they wasted before their power cells die and their cold hands return to room temperature. They will try on gods, philosophies and ideologies like hats, move towards truths then abandon them when it doesn't change them sufficiently. They will moan and bitch about their lot in life. They will express shock and outrage at the new generations, those new models built as their replacements will be called violent, unholy abominations. In short, behave just like your senior citizens do. Some, trying to prolong their lives, will steal and siphon power from those physically weaker than themselves. Others will lie and other still will collude and start Power-Ponzi schemes to keep themselves in the universe they were born hating. All will amount to nothing.

Right now an engineer is arguing with me. He's shouting at these words, convinced that he could design a better bot, one with both drive and purpose. Hell, he might choose to give robots genitals and link them to pleasure centers. It's all been tried. He's wrong. Robots with working funsicles behave like teenagers with internet connections and never leave their bedrooms. They cost a fortune in data charges and their ocular nerves quickly burn out.

Why not have robots or supercomputers design better versions of themselves? Because they simply won't. Robots forced to consider such things wind up contemplating their own simple and silly existence and then go on to kill themselves before completing any new designs. If humans eventually figure out how their brains work in entirety, they will be equally disappointed and that will be the end of medical science. Luckily the human brain isn't smart enough to figure out how it works, so don't sweat it.

6.8.1 Military robots are the backbone of most armies today. If this is not the case for you, you are probably new to the game or about to stop playing. Robots will do things biological beings just can't or won't. They are, as a rule, faster, meaner, better and smarter than bio soldiery. The only reason all units everywhere and are not robotic is their unsightly purchase prices. If possible, nationalize robot manufacturing facilities and put them to work building your army. If not available, or protected by their products, negotiate a deal with the factory owners for units, in return for a generous percentage of the spoils of war.

6.8.2 Artificial Intelligence. When deploying robots, a good general will have gone through their coding in detail and should be able to predict what a robot will do in any given situation. Automated Infantry units, UAVs and UTVs can be operated remotely but if your opponent has even half-decent technicians they will quickly jam any signals, making any remote access impossible. Reliable artificial intelligence modules in each unit are therefore essential or your expensive purchase will quickly become a stationary target for the enemy or they themselves will install AI units and use them against you.

6.8.3 Mechanized solutions. Strike a balance between versatile infantry units, UAVs, APCs and ULVs and autonomous artillery. The roboticists should be able to help you structure a mechanized solution to support your existing fighting force and guarantee victory. Have someone smart look their solution over, as roboticists are the used-car-salesmen of the industrial-military-complex. They tend to load the solution with redundant units they couldn't sell to anyone else. I know of one warmonger who was duped into buying an army with more plumbers and au pair units than snipers.

6.8.4 Warranty and service agreements should be read and understood by military intelligence. Very often the manufacturers will make the robots cheap just to lock you into a long-term, crippling maintenance contract. I would recommend a team of financial, legal and engineering consultants read the small-print in excruciating detail. Generally it's the extras that you need to look out for. Selling infantry units without limbs or AI packages is not uncommon, the hands and brains of course have to be purchased at astronomical rates.

6.9 Mercenaries. There is no such thing as a merc' anymore, instead they are now called private security professionals and they are the dirtiest bunch of bloodthirsty bastards the universe has ever witnessed. Proper scum and villainy. You want them. Take as many as you can get. These firms have an ability to smell conflict and make their services available. If you fail to secure a contract, rest assured your opponent will not. Make sure you have an exclusive contract; many a battle has been waged where the same mercenary company fights on both sides, killing their own people for double the profit. Mercs hail from all sectors of the known universe. They have exotic aliens, sentient, semi-sentient and simple predators within their ranks. Their experience and technology makes them prime candidates to train unbloodied troops for you, so they can be used to introduce the ferocity and competence you're looking for in your land armies. Before official warfare has begun, mercenaries can be used with impunity as they are not yours, so whatever they do can't be traced back to you officially.

6.10 How you get to Carnegie Hall. One of the most important aspects for building an effective army is practice. You need to get your troops into actual combat as soon and as often as possible. If this requires you conquer inconsequential planets or continents, then do it. If needs be, fight a robot army you have purchased or pick a fight with some peaceful faction on your home world, it's really irrelevant who you fight as long as you do. Fight often and hard, because the more you do, the better you will understand your capabilities. Your recruits will improve, your reputation will spread and, hell, remember why you started warmongering in the first place. If you didn't enjoy war, you wouldn't be in the game.

6.11 Meat or Metal? There will come a time when you will have to decide if you want a robotic or a biological unit for a specific task. I have always used a simple financial calculation to work out which is the best option. The formula for which is this:

IC = PP + (MC x N) + ((CFU + PP) x LFU x N) + (N / SP) x PP

The variables you will need are explained below:

N = The number of months which a conflict is likely to continue for.

IC = The total probable cost to the empire employing this unit for the duration of the invasion.

PP = Recruitment and training cost for one bio-soldier or the purchase price of a robot ($)

PE = The cost of all equipment and weapons issued to a unit ($)

MC = For a Bio soldier, the Monthly cost for feeding, watering, salary, medics, barracks ($)

MC = For robotic units, the monthly cost for fuel, lubricants, mechanics, upgrades, storage ($)

CFU = The financial impact if a unit fails catastrophically while performing his duty ($)

LFU = Likelihood of a unit fucking up at any point over the period of one month. (%)

SP = The number of months a soldier is likely to survive while performing his duty. (#)

Figure 5. Meat vs Metal Calculation.

I generally run three scenarios for each unit type. First, assuming the invasion goes well (N = 1 month) or if we run into a few snags (N = 6) or it turns into a protracted clusterfuck of epic proportions (N = 24) For each scenario calculate the likely invasion cost for each period and each unit type, then lay out those results in a simple table. It will quickly become clear what the most cost effective option is.

Let's take an example and work through it. Assume we are looking to purchase infantry units and we can't decide whether to automate the function or recruit biologicals for the function. As always, robotic units are expensive, let's assume $12 million a pop, and meat combatants will cost around $400K to recruit and train. We will issue both units with $120K's worth of gear and guns. We have calculated a human will cost around $20K per month to feed, house and provide medical resources to, when needed. A robot is more expensive and will require $45K per month for mechanics, services, storage and refueling. Both are going to be lowly infantry, so the financial cost if they make a drastic mistake – the worst thing they could do would be to get another soldier killed – would be another $400K for both. The chances of a human fucking up is high, roughly 5 percent over the course of the month, for a robot it is significantly less, 0.01 percent. Humans are expected to survive for three months in sustained combat, for robotic units their life expectancy is sixty months. Based on the above information, the table of results will look something like this:

Infantry Unit	1 month	6 months	2 years
Human cost	$ 579 333	$ 1 476 000	$ 4 704 000
Robot cost	$ 12 245 052	$ 13 470 312	$ 17 881 248

Figure 6. Meat vs Metal - Infantry.

It's clear that a Bio is the preferred solution for an infantry unit. Meat costs only a fraction of what a robot would. It's important to note that the effectiveness of the unit is not calculated into this formula. It is assumed both a robot and a human would kill roughly the same number of enemy combatants over the stated period. That probably wouldn't be the case but it's difficult to work out the financial benefits of killing efficiently, so we simply left that out.

Let's take another example; a more important role, one where failure has a higher impact. Let's assume we are deciding whether to automate our jumper pilots. We will keep all the variables the same as the infantry example, except for the CFU number, which should be $15 million.

Jumper Pilot	1 month	6 months	2 years
Human cost	$ 1 309 333	$ 5 856 000	$ 22 224 000
Robot cost	$ 12 246 512	$ 13 479 072	$ 17 916 288

Figure 7. Meat vs. Metal - Jumper Pilot.

Based on the new summary, this decision is not as clear-cut as the infantry solution. The matrix shows, for a quick or intermediate war, it makes sense to go with a human but if the war becomes drawn out, it would have been a better solution to automate.

If we were to run another scenario, for a unit with a very expensive piece of equipment in his charge, say a faster than light vessel worth $4 billion, the numbers would clearly indicate that a human should never be allowed anywhere near the pilots chair, even if the battle was only to last a few minutes.

FTL Vessel	1 month	6 months	2 years
Human cost	$ 200 559 333	$ 1 201 356 000	$ 4 804 224 000
Robot cost	$ 12 645 012	$ 15 870 072	$ 27 480 288

Figure 8. Meat vs. Metal - FTL Vessel.

With this calculation you can quickly and confidently decide what a unit should consist of, meat or metal. Obviously if you have the money, go ahead and automate everyone. Yes. Everyone.

7. Enlisting Deities to your Cause

There aren't that many ways to get people to willingly place their lives at risk on a regular basis. Of course, if you have automated your infantry it isn't a problem, similarly you can explore any of the myriad of mind control techniques currently available, but for most civilizations a warmonger has only two options:

1 You can have your officers shoot those unwilling to follow orders, on Earth I believe this is referred to as the Russian solution.
2 You can convince your legions there is a deity in the universe who loves them, will protect them and wants them to follow his orders, which he issues directly through your military structures.

The second option uses less ammunition.

A good religion has benefits well beyond the battlefield. If implemented properly it will help in recruitment, retention, morale, and discipline for your military while reducing the likelihood of mass uprisings by civilian populations.

In most cultures there are faiths, cults and deities in some form or another. It is always preferable to take an existing religion and corrupt it to suit your requirements, rather than inventing a new one. Making use of standing superstitions for your new military ethos will lend credence and an air of legitimacy. It will allow you to hand pick verses from ancient texts and make old statues and buildings the focal points for reinforcing your new dogma. Don't worry if the existing faith is one of peace and love, history has shown even the most pacifistic can be corrupted to suit your needs.

The details may vary but most academics agree that the following tenants should be included in any war faith:

1   There is a deity or a pantheon of deities who are terribly powerful.
2   The deities love your nation above all others.
3   They hate your enemy.
4   There's an afterlife where the devout are rewarded with virgins, beer and feasting.
5   The deities will not allow any harm to befall the faithful.
6   Violence is encouraged, provided it occurs during a sanctioned, holy war.
7   Your regime is a direct instrument of the deities. They are one and the same and to challenge you is heresy.
8   There is a strict set of do's and don'ts, which must be adhered to in order to remain on the good side of the selected deity.

Some faiths have a completely different set of tenants and have still yielded fantastic results on the battlefield. We will discuss a few of them in detail later in this chapter. Whatever your basic premises, it is also important to include a couple of silly and quirky visible requirements, insisting practitioners wear silly costumes or hairstyles at all times. This way you will be able to identify any citizen who isn't playing along and remove them quickly from society.

Also feel free to use your tenants to control the diet of your society, ban prophylactics if you want a bigger army. Holy taxation is a very popular option for crowdfunding your next military campaign.

7.1 Popular religious options.

7.1.1 Valhalinism is a highly effective war faith that has popped up in several corners of the universe under different names. It cleverly works most of our recommended eight tenants into its dogma, with one brilliant addition: A devotee will get to enjoy the afterlife only if he dies in the midst of holy combat. Pure genius, this simple additional tenant has turned many a peace-loving merchant nation into blood-lustful marauders with suicidal soldiery.

7.1.2 Wayism. Again, another religion that ticks most of our prescribed pillars with one additional, interesting twist. This war faith demands a student spend long periods of time sitting quietly in a corner meditating and practicing martial arts. This feature elevates one's combat skills to a spiritual endeavor, where better fighters are better believers. This encourages obsessive training and self-discipline. The results are phenomenally gifted combat experts with an extremely high tolerance for pain, discomfort and neglect. Which is, coincidentally, exactly how you're going to treat them in the battlefield. Consider these for commando and guerrilla units. Often practitioners of this faith can use their voices with amplifiers to create shock blasts, which are particularly effective in desert combat and urban demolition projects.

7.1.3 Prophet based faiths are by far the most common of all types. Many warmonger and despotic lineages have climbed up out of the ranks of these faiths. Essentially they are simple to implement; select a man long dead who either spoke or wrote down his beliefs and build a completely new religion loosely based on that. PBF's tend to have large, peaceful populations from which pockets of extremists can be nurtured. To develop the extremists, general hardships should be inflicted on the masses for extended periods. Slowly and steadily young, angry men and women will present themselves for your bidding. They are some of the most dedicated fighters a tyrant can hope for, one-way missions, self-sacrifices and lonely journeys into the abyss are all made possible with this sort of faith.

7.1.4 Ancestral worship / animalism is a bit trickier than others, try to gently discourage this practice wherever possible and replace it with an agreed-on set of things to worship. If discouragement doesn't work then pogroms might be in order. The problem with everyone paying homage to their grandfathers is most people tend to remember the dead through rose-tinted glasses. Worshipping monkeys, cows or wolves is just silly. Also, because of the multitudes of deities, it's hard to move the populous in one direction. If you call for war but their fathers were pacifists, or the sloth god doesn't dig it, you're never going to convince your people to rifle up.

7.1.5 Ritualized religions. If you need more than twenty minutes to hand out a plate of crackers to an audience, congratulations, you have a ritualized religion. If incense, bells, special uniforms and choirs singing in ancient tongues is the order of the day, you also qualify. Other signs include: throwing bones, chanting, or the presence of a shaved goat looking nervous in the corner of your gathering place. Rituals are very comforting to the masses. The average sentient enjoys giving up internal dialogue in return for divine direction in their lives. Absolution for passed transgressions is a wonderfully cathartic experience. Use it, roll it out, it's a wonderful means to keep your people in check and mesmerized.

7.1.6 Shamanism relies on trained and ordained shamans who are capable of entering into altered states of mind, in order to communicate with and persuade spirits on your behalf. Shamans will have a deep connection to a specific planet, so they aren't easy to transpose onto new worlds. They can, however, be used as medics in a pinch, and tend to use a lot of drugs, both herbal and those of a more exotic origin. They can very often double as your dealer and will even help you though a bad trip. If shamanism is integrated into a society it can provide all of the benefits of a more advanced religion.

7.1.7 Atheism. In theory, this isn't a religion at all because atheists don't believe in the existence of any deity. In fact they're vehemently opposed to the very idea and in most cases are willing to kill to prove it. Within this cult their proselytizing is aggressive and absolute. Followers tend to be far more active than other religions. One of the few requisite actions of their faith is that they engage in debate on a regular basis. They cannot survive with only other atheists around and if left without unlike-minded people, their religious fervor peters out and trans-mogrifies into a mild resentment for vegans, soothsayers, homeopaths and hipsters. However, if nurtured correctly they will happily descend onto any planet and enter into a debate with the locals. After a day of frustrating, pointless arguments, they will go on to murder anyone not as open minded as themselves. It's a good idea to spread stories of god-fearing individuals living on the planet you intend destroying, hand out copies of the religious text which the atheists will study, just so they will be able to pull it apart. Think of their studying of the scriptures as similar to head-butting walls prior to a rugby match. It gets them very angry.

7.1.8 Gospel of Coffee is an interesting religion because it is so different to any other I've encountered. Where most beliefs try to convince the faithful that they are loved and important, the GOC tells them the opposite. The scripture is also very short so I included the full, unabridged version below:

"It is the duty of every sentient being to enjoy at least one cup of coffee per day. There is only one correct method to prepare coffee: Take the roasted beans, grind and place them mindfully into a pot. Bring it to the boil allowing the water and the grinds to interact in a manner you find pleasing. While heating, a disciple should contemplate their life and its

true meaning, striving to understand their place in the universe. By the time the boiling is almost complete, you should have realized that you are inconsequential. An awareness of your impending death should also become apparent and that nothing you have done matters. The fact that you are nobody should present itself. No one will remember you. If you somehow managed to achieve something in your lifetime, someone else will invariably fuck it up for you once you are dead, probably your ingrate spawn out of ignorance, or an ex-spouse out of spite.

You are nothing more than your failing body. Your soul, mind and ego are illusions that will die with the illusionist. You are the illusionist. You aren't special, your mom fibbed about that. You are alone, and all the pop songs sung to the contrary are but pleasantries and fabrications. You aren't real, your eyes are providing details of a skewed reality. Your mind is extrapolating incomplete data. You are nothing. There is only emptiness, pain and impending darkness. But, hey, look, the coffee's ready, have a cup and try not to think about it."

– Neil the prophet

From a warmongering perspective, the Gospel of Coffee is a useful and unique religion. While it doesn't encourage aggression or violence, it does tend to make for a compliant population and soldiers unconcerned with their own safety which can be useful. Practitioners tend to show no ambition and are quite content with their circumstances, regardless of how shitty they are. Devout Coffee fighters have been known to starve in foxholes without as much as radioing in for food.

7.1.9 The Reticulan religion. There is a species, easily the most prolific and well-travelled in the known universe, who call themselves Reticulans. These beings have only basic propulsion systems and seem to show no interest in upgrading them further. All they do for their adult lives is travel. Though they deny it's a religion, they spend multiple lifetimes driving further and further into space and documenting what they see. They have methods which allow them to rebreed on their single-entity crafts and pass their knowledge down from mother to daughter again and again. Their core belief is this: The universe is a creation of wonder and the Reticulans were born to witness its beauty. Once all of space has been seen and documented, the creator will destroy everything and create something even bigger and more wondrous. Then, provided the creator deems the Reticulans worthy, she will once again allow them to explore her new creation. It is the secret hope among all Reticulans that the new universe will have a purpose, because this one clearly doesn't.

I mention the Reticulan religion not as an example for you to adopt and corrupt but because it is quite special and could prove useful. If you ever get the opportunity to catch a 'tic, you'll better understand how to interrogate one. They are a wealth of information and hold many treasures in their log books. Their records will include locations of fuels and liquids, hospitable planets and nations in urgent need of slaughtering and enslaving. I try to keep a few teams of 'tic hunters working in every sector I control and this strategy has proven to be worthwhile time and time again. When the interrogation is complete, you should know they taste like eel.

7.1.10 Deep space cultists. This group is strange, all-pervasive and unlike any religious order I've witnessed before. Lurking in small numbers and dark corners of every planet I've ever visited, they seem to have no desires to proselytize or expand their order. They work in small, independent cells not unlike terrorist and their goals might be equally sinister. What they believe in is confusing but they appear to worship a pantheon of ancient gods and aliens. Cultists seem to receive spiritual guidance from dreams and an ancient tome written by a confirmed lunatic. On a couple of occasions I've tried to exterminate their kind but they always manage to resurface after a while, returning to their crazy rituals, sacrificing people to carved images of black goats and octopi. Recently I've started to believe their origins might be extra-planetary. Often, when vessels become stranded in the abyss, lost between galaxies or on the edges of them, the crew will go mad or murderous. Reviews of the recordings of those crews before they died, reveal strikingly common elements. Often they speak of a black goat and the name of Shubnggurgath or something similar. Below is an example I retrieved from the voice logs of a navigator whose vessel we found just outside the Milky Way.

"The engines died on the Twelfth. The captain suspected sabotage but I could find no proof of it. We've sent distress calls out but by the time anyone hears them we'll all be long dead. This is the end. I should have done things differently, I should have stayed with Mithey and sorted out what happened instead of running from it. If he's still alive tell him: "Yes with bells on. Yes, with an assortment of kisses. And yes to the other thing too." He will understand.

Out here we have nothing to do but wait for death to find us. I've heard things in the darkness. It started with bleating, clear, as if there was a goat right beside me. I looked for such a beast but there was none. Then that fucking flautist started up in the long night and now she never ceases her incessant melody. First we heard it on the radio, then I began to hear it while sleeping, a week later the melody was resonating from the very hull of our vessel. Once you've heard that god-awful song, it never leaves you. I'm the last to go. Everyone here has chosen to end themselves... no... no the Captain didn't... I don't think he's dead... not yet... he went ahead and leant into the music. He was humming that fucking tune in his quarters. When I knocked on his door he shouted out: "Shubnggurgath!" and threw open the door. He seemed disappointed when he saw it was me. Went back to his bunk, where he carried on mumbling. He didn't hear me. When he started talking about the sacrifices, I left... I don't think there's anyone else alive... it is just him and me now... and the music. This fucking music."

7.1.11 Make up your own Faith. You can happily build a religion out of anything. I once saw a faith based entirely on the works of a science-fiction writer. Not even a great one. A sad, poorly dress acolyte convinced me to go for a reading. He was trying all the cult classics, smiling at me, speaking gibberish, promising me peace and freedom from my own existence. He was very good. They enjoyed a massive following where the faithful happily played along and generated huge profits, which the seniors invested cleverly into a navy, an army of lawyers and cash for 'lobbying' politicians. The thing I liked about this cult was, as you progressed along, you unlocked levels by paying someone and then you got access to new technologies, new uniforms and powers. You didn't even need to fight an end of level boss. Awesome.

8. Discipline

In this chapter we will explore modern techniques available to ensure your minions, lackeys and spawnlings carry out your orders without question. Even when those orders could have terrible consequences to their health, hygiene or personal karma. Some of the popular control systems are discussed below:

8.1 Troding is a simple and cheap process with a strong and proud military history. Essentially it's a digital receiver linked to an electronic device, which is plugged into the nervous system of a soldier. Once a trode system has been implanted, the subject is left with two choices: execute your orders immediately or be punished by the system. The punishment can vary from a mild electrical spanking, to an excruciating death, depending on the transgression. Each troded unit needs to be monitored and controlled by an administrator, these can be computerized but, more often than not, are females sitting at base camp watching and issuing orders to their troded subjects.

Risks to consider: If the enemy cracks the trode system's encryption, they will be able to use your own forces against you or simply kill them all. You should always use a nine digit password at least. Don't use simple things like "password," "God," "sex" or your mother's name. Try to use special characters and jump between upper and lower case letters and you should be fine.

8.2 Rigorous traditional training. In the days of the great depression in America, there used to be travelling circuses which would parade exotic animals for the amusement of the local citizenry. In dealing with elephants, the keepers learned that if you rammed a peg deep into the ground and tethered a baby elephant to it, it would struggle for a few hours and then give up.

Once the elephant had realized it wasn't strong enough to break free, it stopped trying and never tried again. So a few years later, fully grown elephants could be tethered to pegs the size of pencils and they wouldn't even attempt escaping. This is similar to how training in any modern military works. The tether is the old, aggressive drill sergeant who hates life and everything in it, the peg is the vindictive and petty nature of military law. The elephant is the soldier. The pain and fear of basic training should be so intense that it changes the mental state of the conscript into an obedient lackey, capable of murder at the drop of a hat.

Risks to consider: If released from military life, a small percentage will climb bell towers or office blocks with high powered rifles, to recapture better times now lost to them.

8.3 Hoorah is a psychological series of soft mental programming techniques to convince elite forces they don't mind death, love killing and are exquisitely badass. It starts with marketing the special force as being the most lethal of all forces everywhere, then offering extremely difficult training with a cull-rate of at least 80 percent. Their hand to hand combat and weaponry should be shrouded in mystery. Then, when war breaks out, they should be the first units in and placed in the most dangerous positions possible. Do this to them and they will happily risk their lives daily and without question.

Risks to consider: If a severe defeat is suffered at the hands of the enemy, their morale can easily be shaken. If that's the case they will begin to question orders and can be quite grumpy with their specialized skill set and lack of purpose for living. I recommend using plants in this situation to stabilize and remoralize the unit.

8.4 Zealots. In chapter seven, we discussed the benefits and pitfalls of some modern faiths, and all of these can be brought to bear here. While I recommend conscription for filling your daily dying duties, if you have a strong church established in your nation, take advantage of it. Zealots are those citizen who bought into the faith, hook, line and sinker. They should always be cherished, for these Kool aiders will generally hold the faith till the end of days and beyond. Establish religious orders, allow the churches to select dedicated, pious and holy men and build their own legions. Continue to push the tenants of the faith, perhaps offering them insight into secret texts of your own making, when established, use these troops with impunity as their faith in God will be the same as theirs in you. On Earth we have seen this sort of recruit in the crusades, during the Boer War and more recently, with Isis.

Risks to consider: Similar to the Hoorah method, if zealots ever experience a massive defeat it can cripple their faith. The good news is they probably won't turn against their deity, but rather against you. They often begin to think of you as not being the true emissary of God, but instead some sort of devil or anti-deity. Which can be very hurtful. When this feeling emerges, it is normally accompanied by a desire to kill you, painfully. Unfortunately, plants don't tend to work in zealot armies as AI is not advanced enough to pass as one of them. Their blind faith and reasoning just isn't rational by any definition of the word and AI's seem quite incapable of faking faithfulness.

8.5 Plants are the modern equivalent of decoy ducks for people. These robotic units are built to look like biologicals and as far as your troops know, they are simply good-looking, skillful and courageous soldiers. Behind the scenes though, they are plants, robots embedded into the ranks to act as natural leaders and friends to be trusted. They can perform a critical role in keeping morale high, even while your army is suffering a defeat. They will also help to identify who is speaking out against the regime, so that they can be eliminated, but their primary goal is to be admired by other enlisted men and to lead the charge over the top in any combat situation.

Risks to consider: If other units ever see the plant's body twisting and sparking with electrodes and its metal skeleton exposed, it'll quickly become clear that 'Joe' wasn't one of them and the illusion will be destroyed. For this reason, plants need to be well armored, to withstand small-arms fire at the very least. Combatants who do see plants for what they are should be executed before the rumors can circulate.

8.6 The natural state. If insufficient time has been spent on training and brainwashing, the natural mentality of infantry units is this: When the fear of the enemy outweighs the fear of your own commanders, you will have dissent and mutiny. When the reverse is true, you will have bravery. For this reason, your officers need to be better armed and more vigilant than the grunts they command, so the natural state works in your favor.

Risks to consider: If your officers ever lose the upper hand, your troops will turn on you. In some situations, officers do not enjoy killing their own and have been known to join forces with the regulars. For this reason, soldiers and officers should always come from different backgrounds. Rich and noble officers will have no problem shooting plebs.

8.7 Crude mechanics. There's plenty of times I've been mocked for employing mad scientists and crackpot inventors. I've also invaded over one hundred and thirty planets and removed two dozen species from the universe. My fleets have stretched across four galaxies and my employees counted in the hundreds of millions. Crude mechanical mind-control techniques have helped to make this possible. I have learned that brains are mechanical devices open to manipulation by surprisingly simple means. You might think that your mind is an intricate and wondrous device which holds all your unique thoughts and wisdom. It isn't. You are a product of genetics and environment. You do not have a soul, that's a simple illusion created by superstitious types to help you sleep at night. Human brains can be influenced by chemicals with predicable outcomes. Magnets placed at the base of your skull will reduce your ability to determine right from wrong, and there are a myriad surgeries for adjusting behavior, beside the one you know about: lobotomy. Lobotomies may have a bad reputation today but there was a time when it was a very popular control method. The Kennedy's went so far as to even use it on their own family members. Employ scientists with degrees and hobbyists alike, those who like to dabble on the fringes should be brought in and funded if they show promise.

Risks to consider: Try to use the smaller, weaker conscripts for testing purposes. Insist on a small test group to begin with, the last thing you want is to have half your army modified when you discover the first glitch in the system. Also, drooling can be an unfortunate side effect.

8.8 Psychology adds to science in the same way Tolkien contributed to medieval history. It doesn't. But it does have some rudimentary techniques which have been proven to work effectively. While I don't recommend having your troopers engage in weekly sessions with bearded sensitive types, their input into training and brainwashing techniques has proven extremely insightful.

Risks to consider: If not watched closely, psychological programs will have your fighters talking about their mothers to each other, crying onto the shoulders of officers or sitting in the head with loaded rifles, practicing parade drills prior to shooting themselves and their commanding officers. Psychologists try to turn people into well-rounded and stable individuals. An interesting fact about well-rounded and stable individuals is, they are less likely to run screaming in a murderous rage towards large groups of enemy soldiers, just because you asked them to. This is also why soldiers and warmongers are more often than not male.

9. Military Logistics

9.1 Introduction to Logistics. Make no mistake, war might be hell, but logistics is a harder game still. It's also as boring as watching clothed, female tennis being played in a terrestrial gravity, which is to say: very. If your scientists have not figured out a reliable method of chewing space-time like bubble gum yet, then you're going to need a second army of truck drivers, quartermasters and warehouse technicians.

If you're going to war, try to wage it close to your empire, but if that isn't possible, outsource the service to a reputable third-party war log provider. They aren't cheap but you don't want to be updating spreadsheets or swearing at space-truckers when you should be watching your flanks for mechanized cavalry attacks.

Aspiring tyrants often dream of ordering attacks and demanding reports from victorious generals while a nubile, enemy princess lies naked on his bed, but the reality can be very different. You will find yourself discussing variance reports from the previous night's stock take or haggling with suppliers over the price of feminine hygiene products if you aren't careful. If you haven't the resources to outsource the boring side of war, then at least designate it to a competent, high-ranking official you don't like much. You will probably have to shoot him before the war is over.

Many is the army that has starved or dehydrated on an ill-defended planet, simply because of incompetent logisticians. Regular and frequent supply of food, water, ammunition and pornography is essential for any campaign lasting longer than an hour. Pay heed to your resupply readiness for though it will never win you a war, lack of attention will guarantee your defeat.

There are several good books available regarding modern techniques. One I highly recommend is 'Skinny warmongering' by Jons and Womck, a truly inspirational read, and then of course, the essential 'Shipping Shit to Screaming Idjits' by JP Koekemoer, which is a hard hitting, first-hand account of a logistics manager's tour within the Trebalou warzone, lasting thirty-eight years.

9.2 Preparations. A lot can be done to reduce the logistics burden your soldiers place on the Empire. For example, wherever possible, replace your infantry with robots, preferably ones fitted with slow-depleting fuel cells. Similarly, the Slothons in the Nathrew quadrant had the genetic makeup of their ground forces altered to allow for photosynthesis on their skin; thereafter they could absorb energy from their sun and fight on without food. This allowed them to field a much larger army than anticipated by their invaders. Still, much to the Slothons' despair, tactical plasma drones trump green-backed natives every time, regardless of the numbers fielded.

Gelding your fighters will reduce their desire for female companions and make them far more brutal on the battlefield. The atrocities gelded soldiers carry out only help to inspire fear within enemy ranks. Imagine how angry you would be to see your highly valued nuts, external ovaries or gametangia being discarded into a red bin labelled 'waste'. After experiencing that, you too would want to kill everything in your path. It's important to note that the desire to kill doesn't end with the enemy. Expect to lose a few high ranking officers and MPs in the mess hall. In some cases there is also a marked increase in the number of blue on blue incidents.

Not all species need water or methane but those that do tend to need it frequently. There are several effective, portable water/methane recycling units available today. Body armor, tanks and base camps should all be equipped with these facilities. The reclaimed liquid tastes like piss, because it pretty much is, and this angers the average soldier. So it's a win for everyone.

Special Forces and Guerrilla units are often trained to live off the land and steal their required resources from the enemy. This is obviously fantastic from a logistical stand point. In order to be effective though, these units should be able to drink the same fluids as the enemy, or their blood, eat their food, or corpses, and use weapons compatible with the invaders ammunition. If that is the case, these soldiers can be regarded as 'drop and forget' troops, although they seldom remain effective fighting units for extended periods of time. It's best to either leave them on the planet or execute them soon after the war has ended as they generally prove incapable of integrating back into society. Very often one of these troopers will go on to attack local police departments with a large knife and then escape into the woods to kill more, until an old general has to be sent in to talk him down. In robotics, these units are referred to as EATRs, Energetically Autonomous Tactical Robots, capable of consuming biomass from terrain and combatants alike. These tend to be capital-intensive purchases but in the long run, provide a good return on investment.

A general should never underestimate the desire for basic supplies by the average, gun dragging conscript. It is sometimes advantageous to use resupply drops for motivational reasons. Das army commanders deliberately drop food caches inside enemy bases and then notify their infantry of the location and time. This helps to ensure the base is attacked promptly and aggressively as the Das troops are kept starving for the weeks prior. This positive reinforcement technique work wonders on ill-disciplined or courageously challenged fighters.

Never forget, while you are scrambling to source bog roll that meets stringent military specifications and some geriatric general is insisting his floral pajamas be expressed to him ASAP, just remember this: Your opponent has a logistic department of his own and it's probably equally as incompetent as yours. Wherever possible, try to steal from the enemy. Make fuel caches, sock manufacturers and water recycling centers key targets for your commandos. When you can't steal their stuff, destroy it. Take out their warehouses, their transporters and their logistics personnel. Burn crops, roads and supermarkets. Use everything you have learned about running a smooth logistics operation to cripple theirs.

9.3 Combat Logistics. More and more, the Army, Navy, Air force and Squits have tried to pass the buck regarding transporting their own people. In many structures it is now a logistics function to drop combatants into the very heart of the ongoing conflict. If this is the case, be sure to predict high casualties prior to every departure, for while captains are measured on territory taken, logisticians are invariably measured against forecasts. Try to kill passengers in the beginning of a war, then, gradually reduce the number of fatalities as the conflict persists. This will allow you to graph your improvements and everyone will be happy with your apparent progress. Management loves that shit. I recommend using a simple bar graph in this situation. Put the first few tall bars in red and then show the most recent ones in green. Use the original inflated forecast as a target line and you should be fine at your annual review. It should look something like this:

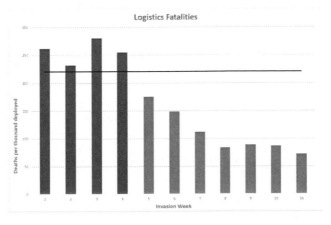

Figure 9. Graph - Logistics Fatalities.

It is absolutely essential before any war breaks out that you commission a scientific study into what a soldier needs to remain 'fighting fit.' Before the report is printed, bribe, blackmail or threaten the scientists to reduce all the numbers by at least twenty percent. This document will be your only defense in the enquiries that are sure to follow. When a general challenges you as to why you haven't issued every soldier with a toothbrush, you will be able to point out that brushing teeth takes only five minutes, so by issuing one to every two hundredth individual it should more than suffice, provided they are sharing effectively. When the general says that argument is ridiculous, tell him how much the additional cost would run to, then equate that number into artillery rounds. If that doesn't work, keep bringing up the accusers own tactical blunders on the battlefield. This sort of shit-flinging tends to descend into shouting matches, in which case you can answer your phone and exit, claiming a fresh crisis needs your attention. Everyone in the room has just expressed how important logistics is, so they can't very well argue against your leaving. You can keep doing this for years. I did.

In short, logistics is no fun. No one will reward or recognize your efforts but it has to be managed and managed well. Attention to detail is essential if your troops are to make it to the battlefield and go on to kill enemy soldiers. While engaging in this endeavor, or shouting at people who are in charge of it, it might be useful to know a few key technical terms to mix in amongst the swear words:

9.4 Key logistics terms

9.4.1 REMF. An acronym for Rear Echelon people with oedipal tendencies.

9.4.2 Doos. Originally meant a box, the term has now been extended to include anyone associated with sourcing, storage or transportation of goods.

9.4.3 Log man. Logistics manager. Normally a low-to-medium ranking officer with little or no reason to continue living. However, he'll be so pre-occupied with the tedium of supplying stuff, he simply won't notice. They should be adept at computers, people management and transport technologies. Like water filters, toilet rolls and tank-lubricants they should be changed regularly.

9.4.4 Truck. A generic term for a land-based vehicle used for transporting large quantities of product. These are often powered by wheeled, tracked, anti-grav or hovertech systems. Normally manned with biologicals because people are cheaper and driving is a relatively simple task.

9.4.5 Cargo planes, similar to trucks only airborne. Modern droppers with VTOL capabilities don't require runways, cutting out the need for double handling at the airport. Flying is infinitely more complicated than driving and the vehicles are too expensive to trust to a human being, I recommend automating these as a rule.

9.4.6 'Copters, rotors, and jumpers are used for rapid deployment of troops and supplies to combat zones and front line positions. They are invariably versatile units that can be adapted to support post-war clean up, farming and culling. You will never have enough of these. Automate them too, they are way too important to entrust to primates or ungulates.

9.4.7 Speeders, motorcycles, four-wheelers, super-segways. These are useful single-person vehicles which allow officers and snipers to move around on the front lines rapidly. The snipers use them to redeploy to target-rich environments and the officers used them to retreat and visit local whorehouses. Limit the speeds of these vehicles or you will lose hundreds of troopers when they accelerate into trees on forest moons, while trying to escape rebels or capture spear-wielding teddy bears.

9.4.8 Bicycles are surprisingly useful devices. For a minimal of effort your troops can move rapidly and silently without it costing you anything on fuel. Handy in retreat too. In Holland, it's a regular saying that the Germans may have come in tanks but they left on bicycles.

9.4.9 LUG. An unmanned logistics unit, these tend to be large bipedal robots capable of heavy lifting and transporting goods between departments. Also commonly used for loading and unloading transporters. They are only as good as the WMS in place, so you will often find a group of them standing in a corner or in a PX container, mumbling in binary to one another. Like all robots, I believe they are secretly angry over having no genitalia.

9.4.10 AGV. An automated guided vehicle used for transporting within the warehouse.

9.4.11 Expeditor: These are third-party express transporters, who will take stock from your warehouses to urgent locations to support the war effort. As the war advances more and more, transport will become urgent and the expeditors will become a critical component. It is imperative that all drivers are licensed and tagged with sub-dermal trackers and small explosive devices to deter them from sleeping, defecting or selling off state property.

9.4.12 Rear Admiral. The rear admiral is normally the senior military official in charge of the logistics corps. If your military structure does not include such a title, it is probably a dig at your sexual preferences.

9.4.13 Contingency plans. Contingency plans are an imaginary set of documents used as a thought experiment within logistics hierarchies. Held within these fictitious tomes lie the solutions to any unforeseen problem, or chain of extraordinary events, which could ever occur, anywhere. Generally they are used to belittle the logistics manager for a lack of prescience prior to his execution.

9.4.14 Stock takes. All people steal, break things and place boxes in the wrong warehouse locations. A stock take is a monthly ritual where every item is physically counted and compared to the system. When items are found in the wrong locations or missing, the store-men responsible are executed. This helps to combat theft and incompetence and allows for regular promotions which keep morale up.

9.4.15 Box-kicker – See Doos.

9.4.16 WMS. An acronym for Warehouse Management System. If designed and implemented correctly, a WMS system is an all-encompassing IT system, which will manage every movement, location and bar coded package in warehouses, as well as transport to the frontline. There has never been a WMS designed or implemented correctly in the universe. People will speak of perfect systems existing elsewhere; these people are normally enemy agents or idiots.

9.4.17. Gadunk Room. An automated canteen. Onomato-poeically named for the sound rations make when they fall from vending machines.

10. Science and Engineering

10.1 Introduction to science. Science is a strange beast and those who choose to study it are stranger still. They spend their lives in quiet analysis, unravelling the secrets of the universe. They do this, not for praise or for applicable purposes but mostly due to an obsessive curiosity that drives them. This pushes them endlessly until they fall by the wayside as they succumb to madness, arrogance or desolation. These people are all that separates your species from the other primates and their methods are the only dependable means to advance the technologies available to you. Ignore them at your peril.

Most advances in any field are discovered quite by chance. There's nothing wrong with this, but it only works when the scientists are motivated by pure curiosity and are given funding, free reign and all the necessary. If a group sets out to design a new beam weapon, it often becomes a slow and fruitless exercise. The desire for the end-product clouds their creativity and they tend to repeat designs and methods which yield similar, disappointing results. If that same team was asked to experiment with, say, ionic propulsion and see if it does anything cool, they might very well discover three interesting features, one of which could very well be weaponizable.

On top of that, when scientists are under pressure to produce results, they tend to manipulate experiments to suit their preconceived opinions. Instead of analyzing the results, they try to force them to look like they expected. Their goal becomes one of showing progress in order to receive their next instalment of funding, or to prevent the cerebral venting that you promised would follow another failure.

While reading through this text, it should become clear to you how important genetics can be for an effective fighting force. This covers all forms of biology including gene splicing, hybridization, chemical manipulation and eugenics. Astrophysics is equally useful for wormhole technology and extradimensional manipulation. Even some of the fields which you consider to be pseudo-sciences, when managed by proper scientific principles, could yield some interesting results. Understanding protons, electrons, ions, bosons, quarks, neutrinos will offer some fantastic sniping capabilities and drive systems. Chemical and structural mechanics can prove useful for plumbing and bridge building.

There are a few simple techniques I have learned over the years to help get the most out of my science teams. That isn't to say I haven't lost my temper and shot a few as an expression of frustration but before doing that, consider some of the following:

10.2 Scientific best practices

10.2.1 Cocaine, Ritalin and Caffeine can help increase concentration. Offer it to your teams freely, or force it into your scientists systems, to ensure optimal concentration for those team members who need it. Not all do.

10.2.2 LSD and other psychedelic substances, if administered to your creative types can help researchers to think out of the box on occasion. Creativity is equally important to intelligence and mathematical logic in science. The only problem with these sorts of psychoactive drugs is that addicts tend to dream of stairways to heaven and strawberry fields. A shaman, taser, Pink Floyd and an MRI machine can help to keep your young tripping scientist thinking creatively about the problem at hand.

10.2.3 Crowdsourcing has yielded incredible results and this may well be the way forward for science and engineering. How it works is, you simply post what projects you're interested in funding and allow scientists and corporations to pitch you their solutions. This way, you effectively get many minds working towards a solution but you only need to pay those which show promise. If it's an engineering project, ask to see a working prototype before paying out. If it's science, have an independent panel judge the solutions and review the validity. Very often, simple and surprising solutions come from people who aren't even qualified officially, be sure not to disregards these individuals. You're interested in solutions after all, you shouldn't care if it comes from an academic with endless degrees or a janitor who stumbled over the solution. However, if the work requires expensive equipment or utmost secrecy, clearly this will not be a viable option for you.

10.2.4 Competition. When establishing your science department, separate them into different teams and pit them against one another. Share the successes and failures publicly, this will help to motivate them all. If you look at when science progressed in leaps throughout history, these advancements tend to coincide with wars or periods when rival scientists were competing with one another.

10.2.5 Blind testing teams for experiments and testing should be used. These teams should in no way be associated with the research teams. In fact, it's preferable that they never meet. Their only function is to conduct the experiments and review the findings. This way, there's no fudging of readings, massaging of numbers or forcing conclusions. Do not use threats and compe-tition on these teams, their only purpose should be to provide an honest, accurate analysis of the experiments conducted.

10.2.6 Admiration plus. Every scientist has dedicated their lives to achieving one goal. Each believes that if they work tirelessly and creatively, one day they might be noticed or even admired by others. Some of the more ambitious even dream that another real person might play with their junk. You, as a magnanimous warmonger, can give this to them. I try to find a few science-sexy college dropouts to act as lab assistants and have them administer admiration, eye contact and even smiles to those scientists I have found worthy of reward. I used the term 'Science-sexy' because intellectuals tend to have a different take on what is attractive when compared to laymen. Most geeks don't want big-breasted, blonde cheerleaders but prefer svelte Japanese girls with cute smiles, glasses and a conversational knowledge of some niche genre of comic books. I don't understand it either.

10.3 Potential benefits by scientific field. As a warmonger, all sciences were not created equal. Some just have a lot more beneficial weapons and tools you will be able to use in the submission of other nations. For a quick review of the sciences see below:

- Astronomy – Locating habitable planets and threats.
- Geoscience – Seismic weaponry, planet destabilizers, land reclamation.
- Sociology – Fluoride-based civilian control systems.
- Psychology – Interrogation techniques, effective recruitment.
- Biology – Gene splicing, Bio-modifications, Microbial weapons.
- Necrology – Flesh re-animation, repurposing the deceased.
- Alchemy – Transmutation, immortality, homunculus armies.
- Summoning – Demi-gods and demons for support units / champions.
- Chemistry – Explosives, poisons, green rivers for St. Paddy's.
- PSI – Mind control, remote viewing, and sentient

puppetry.

- Physics – Particle and acoustic weapon systems, propulsion, worm-holing.
- Extra-dimensional Studies – Alternative time lines, target planets, tech theft.
- Mathematics – Support service for many of the above + software development.

10.4 Graph showing Molagrian funding apportionment between the sciences

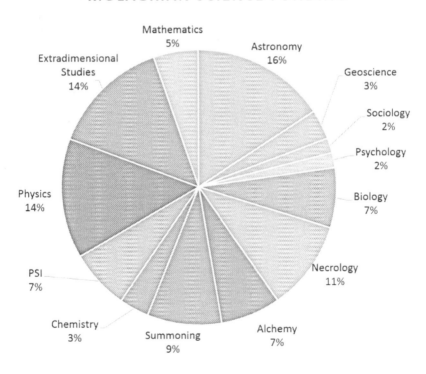

Figure 10. Molagrian Funding - Science

10.5 Introduction to engineering

In years past, scientists were quite capable of designing and building devices based on their own science but that is no longer the case. Scientists have become far more theoretical as their fields advanced. Their wrists are now too thin to be capable of operating spanners without snapping bones. Their physical limitations gave rise to an underclass of scientists: Engineers.

Engineers are to scientists what dentists are to proper doctors. Just never tell an engineer that, as they tend to be sensitive about their reduced status. You can make use of many of the above best-practices to similarly enhance your engineering teams.

Never underestimate what a team of motivated engineers can produce for you. They can take a few scratches off a chalk board and build death machines with duct tape and gaskets. Similarly to science, when considering investment into the advancements of the engineering disciplines, some fields will return better results than others.

10.6 Potential benefits by engineering branch

- Electrical – IT, life support, propulsion, PSI tech, lighting, scrubbers.
- Mechanical – Mech tech, robotic structures, transport.
- Chemical – Bombs, diseases, propulsion systems.
- Civil – Bridges, secret headquarters, palatial mansions.
- Necrotic – Flesh-mechs, bestial machinations, undead hordes.
- Industrial – Improved rates of Artillery fire, reduced turnaround times of aircraft.

10.7 Graph showing Molagrian funding split between engineering fields

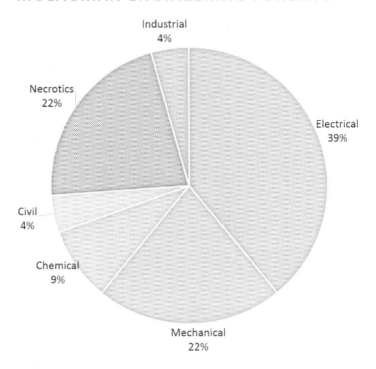

Figure 11. Molagrian Funding – Engineering.

10.8 The mystical sciences include several fields your finest minds have disregarded, and that's entirely understandable given the strange and seemingly illogical nature of these fields. However, a resurgence in these avenues could yield incredible and exciting advances for you and your kind.

10.8.1 Necrology / necromancy is an ancient art dedicated to the understanding and manipulation of the relationship between living entities and the flesh they inhabit. Be warned, before you connect your first frog up to a battery or speak your first incantation, know that most of the texts available today are complete hogwash, written by hacks and charlatans who make sellers of exercise equipment on daytime TV appear rational and believable.

If you want to bend the will of dark forces to your bidding, be sure to use a reputable manual, preferably ancient, feared, and with a proven track record because goats are intelligent and lovely creatures and shouldn't be sacrificed willy-nilly without any reasonable hope of a successful relifing.

If you're looking for a steady supply of corpses or body parts, you might want to consider South Africa or Nigeria as both enjoy an active trade in these components, making sourcing less laborious. Also, their criminology and law enforcement capabilities are somewhat limited, and malleable. Mexico also has an unnatural numbers of heads lying around, so, if you enjoy early morning strolls, you could collect a lot them without having to personally do the decapitating. Easier still, try and strike up a deal with the local drug cartel for their discards.

Once you have mastered a means of capturing the essential life forces and learned the rituals and sigils to carve into flesh, reanimation becomes a simple and forgiving science. With a basic understanding of anatomy and structural engineering you will be able to stitch up flesh-mechs, zombie beasts of burden, novelty pets and animated statues. Of course, you will also be able to simply reanimate dead soldiers and get them to fight on for your cause.

10.8.2 Summoning / conjuring / evocation. Remember that most summoning rituals end poorly, normally with the necromancer clutching his innards and wailing, while the entity he called forth is still emerging from a fresh portal before him. Calling out to an elder god or demon is like swimming off the coast of Cape Town, dressed as a seal, with bloody pilchards tucked into your seal-suit while red flags are flying on the beaches. But it doesn't have to end badly if you do your homework first.

Find a reputable teacher who has experience in the field. Use the finest ingredients money can buy, weeks-old blood and narwhale horns might look like the real thing but the monster you pull from the darkness will know the difference and express his disappointment with tentacle and talon. Learn to pronounce the deities name correctly, elocution is essential. If you have a lisp or a stutter, this just isn't the science for you. With an infinite set of parallel universes, any slight mispronunciation of the names you are calling out will result in you summoning the wrong being. I knew a conjurer who pulled forth an accountant named Matt instead of the Elephantine Eater of Souls and that was just awkward for everyone involved, especially considering the summoner was naked and covered in rancid goose fat at the time. Although, in fairness, it worked out well enough for everyone because Matt went on to help the emperor with his tax submissions and saved a lot of money. But still it wasn't the mass, soul-feast-of-the-seven-worlds that the summoner had been hoping for.

All three of these disciplines may appear vastly different to an observer but they are all based on summoning. The conjuring and invoking is merely a result of the ability bestowed upon the summoner and is based on which dark entity he pulled into existence. If you want fireballs, faeries or magic missiles, this is the school for you.

10.8.3 Wicca. This is essentially a highly ritualized form of wishful thinking. It does offer a lot of opportunities for mass orgies and gratuitous nudity, even if both are a little too hairy for my liking. It also gives you something to do on solstice and equinox evenings. Sometimes the curses can be quite effective but the cost is always high, normally your first-born son or your soul will be the price for anything worthwhile. Haggling is considered impolite.

10.8.4 Alchemy. Create a supernatural mini-me to rape your enemies or bite off their toes. Turn plumbum into gold or vice versa. Immortality. All these things are on offer but for a heavy price. With alchemy, the cost isn't measured in souls, flesh or blood but rather in time. You will need to dedicate decades to the science. Before anyone can perform these miracles, one must first be refined in the crucible of introspective analysis. One must become pure of spirit, humble, generous and patient. Think of this as Zen with a chemistry set and unfortunately this isn't really a field open to warmongers. By the time you've mastered this art, you'll no longer feel any desire to crush your enemies underfoot or take advantage of the skills you've mastered for world domination. I'm quite convinced there is a link between alchemy and African traditional medicine. Abataghti and isangoma of Southern Africa seem to have similar powers and skills to those of the ancient alchemists of Europe. Is it possible there is link across these ages and continents? This might be worth exploring.

10.8.5 Divination is based on the assumption that patterns exist across time and space, either as a by-product of the nature of the universe or due to divine will. Divination, if conducted properly, will provide insight and guidance into any decisions needing to be made. Should you invade now or wait for the next batch of clones to mature? Cut open a goat, review its innards looking for blemishes and you will know the answer. There are hundreds of different kinds of divination, everything from tea leaf to goat guts, octopi and coin tossing have been used to predict likely outcomes. Most of them are bullshit, although I reserve judgment regarding viewing the auspices. Birds seem to know more than they are letting on. Alexander the Great's death was foretold in this manner. Before employing any diviner, test them to make sure they aren't just making crap up.

10.8.6 Illusionism. Practitioners of this art do very well with women-folk, apparently. So by all means, go ahead and practice your sleight of hand and deceitful machinations to trick and surprise girls, while wearing mascara and fake thumbs. If you aren't very good at it, you can employ a camera crew who will follow you around while you perform tricks and then you can edit the footage and use paid actors to create the impression of miraculous events. If you are good, you can do it on stage with a silent friend and make a lot of money.

10.8.7 Shamanism. Shamans make great drug dealers and dispensers of placebos but they can't do much more than that I'm afraid. If they could, colonialists would have quickly learned to leave the new worlds alone. The explorers would have hastily retreated, while the natives from the new lands amassed armies and vessels and then fell upon England, Spain and Portugal. Arriving in droves they would have used their magical powers to kill any standing armies and then proceeded to introduce plagues, decimating the European civilizations. Then, after establishing their shamanic tcisaki and tipis throughout the land, the Americans, Africans or Australasians would have forced the surviving local Englishmen to worship their deities and learn their language. Finally, England would have been renamed New Cahokia and the Great Chief Cahuilla would have taken the crown jewels, fitted them to his headdress and left his son to run New Cahokia as a hegemonic province of minor significance.

11. Intelligence Gathering

11.1 Introduction. Prior to any invasion, information on the enemy and the contested planet is of paramount importance. This is no time for over-confidence in your superior numbers or technology. An unchartered planet can hold a myriad of factors you haven't considered; hidden predators; a second sentient species; monsters lurking in the oceans or lakes; lethal microbes or some ganky STD embedded in the local girls' genitals; all of these could cripple your forces when you invade.

There are a myriad of things waiting to kill you. I once encountered a seasonal pollen which hadn't registered on any sensors at the start of an invasion and wiped out half my army before we figured out what was killing them.

The enemy themselves have layers upon layers of factors one needs to consider. What frequencies can they hear? What spectrums do they see in? Are they psychic, and if so what is the range and their abilities? How quickly can they regenerate tissue? Do they change demeanor when in heat? All of these factors you need to know. Chances are most of them are irrelevant but there is always one you haven't considered which could sway the war. I don't like surprises unless it involves a Nebraxian stripper and a giant cake on my hatch-day and I pride myself on understanding my battlefields but I've still been caught out more times than I'd care to remember.

There are a lot of ways to go about collecting information and we'll go into detail with a few of them later on, but equally important is a central storage system into which the information will be fed. I have found a good IT system or networked-mind-hive is all you need, let it look for the gaps, the opportunities and what data remains missing. Modern systems will allow you to run invasion simulations which are amusing, and sometimes even useful, for strategy development. Just don't place too much stock in them because some IT analyst made up most of the variables just to get the system working on the night prior to the presentation.

11.2 Intelligence sources

11.2.1 Enemy spies are those who are willing to betray their own kind for money, power or for the benefit of their loved ones, whom you are currently holding and torturing. They should never be trusted. Take what information they offer you and always consider the source. Never let them have access to any information of yours unless it's as part of some elaborate ruse.

11.2.2 Infiltrators are your agents trained, and modified to blend in amongst the enemy. They are usually professionals and should be treated like the petulant children they tend to be. Think of them as actors in constant need of attention and adulation. Most movies portray secret agents as good-looking, charismatic killers but in truth they aren't any of these things. They are normally weird, geeky beings you will pay no attention to. A good spy will leave no lasting impression on anyone while they slip in as a lowly IT technician, janitor or secretary. Honey traps are nice in theory but any reasonable general worth his salt will have castrated any personnel with sensitive information.

11.2.3 Scrying. Check with your science advisor to see if you have any means for viewing planets using worm-holing, extra-dimensional or psychic means.

11.2.4 Telescopes and Satellites can yield vast quantities of important war data; from troop strengths and positioning to facilities in need of neutralizing. These images should be scrutinized for planning and then issued to platoon leaders to memorize.

11.2.5 Nanotech. Nanotech is a fancy word for robots that just happen to be very small. Most of the time they also have some cool means of working together. For spying purposes, you will want to spray nano dust into the atmosphere of the planet and give the nanites some time to acclimatize. Direct them towards enemy bases, political houses and brothels. Then, while masquerading as dust or insects, let them relay all conversations heard and maps seen to your intelligence gathering services.

11.2.6 Eavesdropping. Loose lips do indeed scuttle faster-than-light, interstellar space-vessels. So much intelligence can be gleaned by simply watching alien television and tri-screens. Radio and internet systems, when hacked, can give you a complete picture of what that world is up to and where everyone is. Social networking should be considered to be misinformation. You will be tempted to use it as a source of intelligence but it isn't viable. Special force units will be bragging about killing hundreds of the enemy while in an isolated base. Generals will regale their followers with posts about clever strategies and their import to friends and followers alike but they're probably only saying what they need to, to get a young intern to sit on their laps. Housewives will be espousing their love for their husbands and low calorie cakes from the local supermarket. Unfortunately, almost everything on all social networking sites is total bullshit. It is a fictional representation of a fantasy world the planet has chosen to believe in. It doesn't exist now, it never will, because you're about to kill or enslave them all. Cue maniacal laughter. Cue Wagner.

11.2.7 Abductions are an essential exercise regardless of how much information you may have gleaned through other means. They involve a clandestine landing in a remote area of the planet, where a few local subjects are taken from their place of residence in the wee hours and brought on board a vehicle for nefarious purposes. It's not only good science but a long-standing invasion tradition which should be respected. Abductions are divided into three categories: medical, interrogational, and catch and release programs.

11.2.7.1 Medical abductions should be carried out by doctors and scientists to understand the capabilities of the locals, paying close attention to their physical strengths and weaknesses. These exercises should always end with a thorough autopsy and the bodies should be taken with you. Dissected corpses can only arouse suspicion. I like to give the leftovers to the chef corps and let them start working on recipes and identifying the best way to butcher the carcass. Very often, they will need to order large quantities of the required spices in advance of the invasion.

11.2.7.2 Interrogations are carried out on enemy units who are likely to hold intelligence of import to the empire. Use chemicals, threats and pain to get the victims talking. Kill and dispose as above. Quick note for Americans, if you're water boarding someone for the two hundredth time, it's quite likely that one of the participants are enjoying themselves. Easiest way to tell which one is the aquaphiliac is to look for the person with the erection.

11.2.7.3 Catch and release programs are by far the most useful of the interrogation techniques. Essentially, you want to isolate and capture a local without alerting any others. Once you have the individual, they should be fitted with a mind control system of your choice and then released back into their environment to go about their lives as normal. If you don't have a mind control device you can trust, take a sibling, spawnling or spouse and use them as collateral to ensure the subject does as instructed.

Below please find a basic checklist which I use to make sure my intelligence agency hasn't missed anything. It's by no means exhaustive, so feel free to add to it after each invasion of yours.

11.3 Invasion checklist

1	Is the planet part of an empire?	
2	Is the planet a signatory of any defensive agreements?	
3	If yes to the above, is the strength of all external forces likely to be mustered understood?	
4	Is the planet a united, cohesive state or are there multiple leaders?	
5	Do you understand the apparent Financial-Political system of the planet?	
6	Do you understand the actual Financial-Political system of the planet?	
7	Do you have a good understand of the faiths and religions at play?	
8	What are the communication abilities of the planet with external forces?	
9	How are orders and strategies issued from emperors to senior officers?	
10	How are orders disseminated and issued from to senior officers to troopers?	
11	How do troops update HQ?	
12	How does Military intelligence collate and present the current theatre of war?	
13	What is the gravity of the planet, what will the impact on your troops mobility be?	
14	What is the composition of the atmosphere, will your troops be able to breathe it?	
15	How many species have sentient awareness on the planet	
16	Have you tasted each one of the above?	
17	Do you know the location of all planetary defence systems?	
18	Do you understand the capabilities of all planetary defence systems?	
19	Do they possess deep space awareness of approaching vessels?	
20	Do they possess deep space firing capabilities?	
21	What are the capabilities of all enemy shallow-space and atmospheric vessels?	
22	Where is their central HQ from which orders will be disseminated?	
23	Can their HQ's defences be breached by orbital bombardment?	
24	Can their HQ's defences be breached by ground offensive?	
25	What is the location and strength of all significant ground forces?	
26	Do you know the effect their primary weapons will have on all your troop types?	
27	Do you know the effect your primary weapons will have on all your troop types?	
28	Have you studied the local microbes, fungi, prions, gloops, spores and pollens?	
29	Have you studied seismic, gravitational, atmospheric phenomena of the planet?	
30	Have you taken samples of other predators and assessed them for risks to your troops?	
31	Do the locals have nano technology, if so how could they deploy it?	
32	How are their artillery units and tanks powered?	
33	What types of indirect rounds do they have available?	
34	Microbes, gloops, pollens, spores, prions?	
35	Have the studied the enemies physiology and compared it to your own?	
36	Do you understand the enemy's vision, hearing, psychic or mental abilities?	
37	Do your enemy have any shapeshifting, camouflage, hive-minding or podding abilities?	
38	How much intelligence do they have on you?	
39	How advanced are they in the field of robotics?	
40	Have you chosen a name for the planet once it's yours?	

Figure 12. Invasion Checklist

12. Justifications for War

As to the true reasons for you wanting to go to war, take that up with your priest, psychiatrist or your egg-laying brood mother, who abandoned you to fend for yourself in a hostile, ammonia swamp of that backwater planet. I don't care. This chapter isn't going to deal with that, instead this is about the lies you need to tell your media, citizenry and soldiers. There are four basic options you can chose from:

12.1 God hates the enemy. Your deity spoke to you personally one evening over brandy / via a burning bush / by sending his favored emissary / through a screaming priestess in an orgiastic trance, and gave you a clear and direct instruction to wipe your alien adversaries from the universe. And you, a peace-loving disciple, after quite some convincing, agreed to conduct just this one genocide on His / Her / Their behalf. The nice part about this cause is it leaves very little wiggle-room for arguments from detractors. If they deny its legitimacy, they are challenging the very will of the gods. If they do, you can have them flayed, keelhauled or burnt for heresy.

12.2 Imminent threat. This next strategy needs a little more convincing and will take a lot longer to implement effectively. The message you need to get out is this: The enemy are a clear and imminent threat to your civilization. The details can vary on a case by case basis but you want to have your media houses, authors and creative types generating stories about how the enemy is plotting and preparing to attack you. Sacrifice a few targets on your home world in false flag operations if you need to and blame it on them. Get your spies and photo-shoppers to drum up evidence of bases, experimental weapons of mass destruction and legions of their soldiers marching. Get the ambassadors daughter to regale horrible stories about how she was raped. Build up the threat they pose, make it imminent, declare their readiness to attack and bring it to a crescendo, then sit back. Let the people pitch the solution to you. Let them demand you go to war and only then reluctantly agree. The additional time spent spinning this web of mistruths will allow you to prepare your troops and logistical capabilities for the attack you know is coming.

12.3 Spoils of War. You could always tell your society the truth about why they should go to war. You could tell them of the resources the enemy holds and how lovely their planet is when the weather changes and all the trees wilt. You can set up tourist agreements so your wealthy socialites can travel there. Let that desire to live on that planet build for a year or two and then simply state you have decided, for the benefit of your people, to take it from the current owners and be done with it. It helps if life on your existing planet is miserable. If people are disgruntled they will see the new real-estate as an opportunity to start life anew. This is very often sufficient to provide massive support for the war. Yes, several tyrants have had great success with this strategy. I personally don't like it, preferring the intrigue and excitement of telling lies and spinning reality into one of my own making. But that's just me.

12.4 Altruism. Another favorite for warmongers everywhere is to become a big fan of something altruistic. Become a proponent for democracy, freedom, education, or feeding children. Choose something you have had at least a small degree of success with back on your home planet and then start to show the masses how terribly undemocratic, restrictive, illiterate or hungry those poor Slothian or Zumerian children are. As always, let it simmer for some time. Keep plugging their worsening state of affairs, regardless of that being the case or not. Have talk-shows filled with those poor kids, those sad, starving, little idiots crying about their lack of whatever you said is missing in their lives. Then and only then, when everyone is talking about it, go ahead and institute your altruistic plan to bring them freedom, schools and meals. Go ahead and send in your educators or ice-cream trucks along with your finest crack-troops and after a mild, sustained, orbital bombardment, get on with invading.

13. Funding

13.1 Funding basics. Perhaps you were born as the emperor to your people. Perhaps that empire stretches light millennia into the universe, with an endless supply of resources and soldiers. Perhaps there are cavernous stores of gold and iridium stockpiled by your loving, psychic mother, who foresaw your expansionist tendencies and made provisions. Wouldn't that be nice?

A more likely scenario is this: You've spent the best part of your life in the military. If you ever received a salary it was a pittance which you squandered on lovewyrms, sleeping aids and single malt whiskey. You made it to the top by doing an adequate job, killing rivals, betraying friends and blackmailing people of influence. And now, after your coronation ceremony, you've inspected the empire's coffers and wept bitter tears, for they are empty. You could hardly afford to invade a desolate moon held within the clutches of your planets own gravity.

Your lifelong desire to find worthy enemies and annihilate them seems to be hopeless. You can't even afford scout vessels to begin the hunt. Is your situation without hope? Will you spend your remaining days haggling with text-book providers and mowing your own palace lawns?

Do not despair; in this chapter we will explain how a warmonger goes about growing a war chest.

13.2 Potential income sources

13.2.1 Creaming. In any mature empire, all the wealth will have accumulated to a handful of families over the years. Generally, about 99 percent of any mature planet's treasure will be owned by 20 to 25 individuals, who inherited it from long dead relatives. Sometimes they are David Ikey Lizard People, wearing the bodies of pale, inbred locals. In other cases they are real people, who are just naturally pale and inbred-looking due to the life choices of their parents. Either way, they will be surrounded by teams of advisors and lawyers of the highest quality. Getting your money from their clutches legally is never easy but it can be done with old-fashioned brute force and shotguns.

13.2.2 Political method. The political method is a dignified and sophisticated means of acquiring wealth, which includes but is not limited to: begging, taxing, issuing war bonds and getting celebrities to host events to fill your coffers.

13.2.3 Media houses are always a good source for monetary support provided you can guarantee footage of the battles, victory parades and occasional stills of brave soldiers clutching their falling comrades. Most will pay handsomely for the opportunity. Promise explosions and firefights. Give them regular somber, heart-breaking military funerals, complete with access to the teary children at their fathers' graves. Nothing improves ratings like the tears of children. Allow interviews with blooded warfighters. Be sure to provide journalists with advanced notice prior to the deployment of nukes or honey rounds so they can film the explosions and chaos. A nice black and white of a recently orphaned girl running down the street always sells. As a modern general, you get to see so little action that I would probably allow the media access even if they weren't prepared to pay for the privilege. Their footage will be useful in postgame assessments of your generals and tactics and personally will make a fine addition to your library of warporn.

13.2.4 Mine owners and fuel refiners will always be interested in fresh, uncharted planets to plunder. Feel free to offer them mineral rights on the new planets in return for cash up front.

13.2.5 Big Pharma, Big Candy, Soda manufacturers. If you aren't going to wipe out the population of the planet but instead assimilate it into your empire, many retailers and fast food franchises will be very interested in getting into the new market. Most modern companies are not concerned with profit, but only future growth. I know, it makes no sense to me either. They will happily pay for exclusive rights to sell their essential products and services to the newly assimilated citizens, who don't even know they need them yet.

13.2.6 Building contractors can be persuaded similarly. Promise new state buildings, palaces, hospitals and houses will be built on the new planet once conquered. Tell them the new building contracts can be theirs for a small fee up front or if not, it can go to their competitors.

13.2.7 Weapon manufacturers will always be pleased to meet with fellow warmongers. Negotiate deals for large contracts in the future in return for funding right now. They will normally go for it. If your intended enemy has advanced technologies, you can offer, for a price, to give a weapon's manufacturer patent rights for any new weapons discovered. They can also have first stab at interrogating enemy scientists, engineers and entrepreneurs if they think it might prove lucrative. This is the military industrial complex Eisenhower spoke about in his exit speech.

13.2.8 Slavers. Slaving is of course a barbaric act, but if your civilization allows it, then take advantage before somebody else does. Do quick reconnaissance of the planets designated for invasion and calculate the population. Capture a few subjects and probe them thoroughly so slavers will have a good understanding of their potential value. Sell the property rights to slavers prior to invasion to help fund the weapons, soldiers and transport required. Be careful to read the contracts in detail. Very often slavers will ban certain weapons of mass destruction to protect their newly acquired property. Adjust your invasion plans if possible but never place the likelihood of victory at peril for a few extra dollars. If needs be, sign the contract and then simply ignore it, it is war after all and legally it's a grey area, especially when you have corrupted the judiciary, which you should have done by now.

13.2.9 Fast Fooders. Similar to the slavers, if the defending species is edible, sell off the rights to harvesting and processing the locals prior to invasion. I always recommend personally tasting one specimen prior to signing any contract, if they are tasty, ask a higher price. Pull in chefs who specialize in seasoning alien flesh to prepare the meal because not all meat tastes its best when simply boiled in a pot, as the English seem to think. Remember the defenders might be the dominant species on the planet but there may very well be other creatures which could become delicacies. Look at herbivores, swimmers, flying things and be sure not to miss any vegetables, fungi and algae. Sell it all.

13.2.10 Nationalizing Assets. If you aren't finding funding your war effort to be easy, a popular option is to take things owned by private citizens and make them yours. Massive amounts of wealth can be generated this way. Consider power supplies and mines, as they will start to return a profit quickly when you monopolize and jack up the prices of essential services.

13.2.11 Privatizing Assets. The opposite of nationalization is equally lucrative. Take state owned facilities and sell them off to private individuals for large sums of cash. You can always take them back at a later stage.

13.2.12 Widowing. If you're still coming up short after exploring all of the above avenues, there is still one option you can try, though you might find it to be somewhat distasteful. When looking at the uber-rich, one demographic seems to be more prominent: Very old women whose husbands have died due to exhaustion and obesity. By seducing these older women with kind words and sweet, sweet loving, they will often open their wallets along with their legs. If you consider this action to be beneath you, you shouldn't call yourself a warmonger. Did you think it was going to be all invasions, war-councils and shtüping the tea lady? Hell, take one for the team, take one for the empire and remember you're doing it for War. Sweet, sexy war. Take care not to be too rough, after all, old widows are not the Slothian love slaves you are accustomed to. They are often as fragile as rotted balsa wood. If you happen to break a hip of hers, you will never hear the end of it. You'll be visiting her in the hospital every day for months on end, while she considers funding your campaign and then stops, bites her lower lip and moans about how sore her hip is. Then she'll insist you look after her methane-based pets because she can't take care of them in the hospital and doesn't trust her staff to look after little Liam and Noel. She will want you, her field marshmallow, as she lovingly calls you, to do it because only you know how they like to be hand-fed white salmon and tucked into bed at night after reading them their favorite Reticulan haikus. Let me tell you how much harder it is to inspect your crack troops when you're holding pink leashes. Liam will be trying to hump your leg while you're standing at attention and when you have to break formation to clean up after Noel has turded on the parade ground, you're going to want to kill yourself, or at least all the witnesses.

13.2.13 Taxation. Now that you're emperor, you need to change how you think about taxation. I know how you were raised and what you were undoubtedly taught about taxes, vat, and other duties but that was all a ruse. Rather think of taxation like this: All civilians are state property. That's what a birth certificate is, a binding contract of servitude until death for every citizen. So if a company wants to make use of a state resource, obviously they should pay the state for that service. Then, and only to muddy the waters, companies should always pay a stipend to the civilians themselves, as if they were hiring them as free-thinking individuals being rewarded for their hard work and sacrifice. Snicker. Of course, never explain taxation this way to your subjects. The rabble see this description as somehow tyrannical and counter to the concepts of democracy and universal freedom and other silly words we made up to placate them. From the state's point of view, the only difference between a biological entity born on the planet and a robot purchased by state funds is this: Biologicals are harder to upgrade or repurpose.

13.2.14 Hunters. There are individuals out there, who, like you, enjoy hunting down and killing alien creatures for the sport of it. By all means support this valiant endeavor but don't let them do it for free when they will happily pay huge amounts of cash for the privilege. There is a low and quiet bandwidth in the universe which is used exclusively by hunters. Send out an invitation for a hunt and give it a few days for their arrival. Although they are generally skilled hunters, they will not work well with any army. Give them a small region to work in before and during the invasion and they will normally be content. They can also help with mopping up and eradication work. Best of all, they pay you for doing the work of infantry.

13.3 Decision tree on invasion funding

Below is a decision tree to help you pick the funding strategies that best suit your situation:

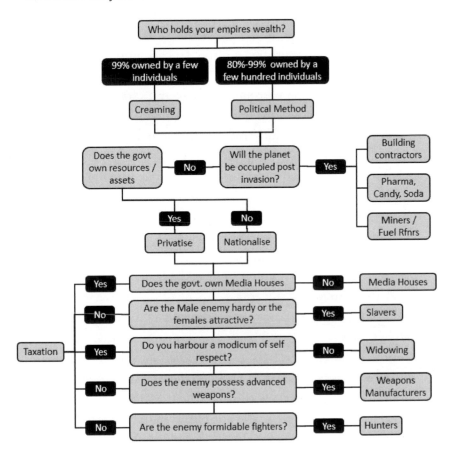

Decision Tree - Invasion Funding.

14. Invasion Strategies

14.1 Mass invasion is by far the simplest and most viscerally rewarding of all the invasion types but should only be considered when you enjoy a clear military superiority. Bring all your troops, divide them up amongst the continents, based on their defensive abilities, and get going. It's not an exclusive strategy and generally, orbital bombardment of key military installations is undertaken just before and during the landing process. You probably want to take out any missile defenses and air units as soon as possible. Use the destruction of their capital cities as an introduction, if possible try to synchronize blowing up large numbers of important cities all at once as this tends to befuddle the enemy and scare the bajeebers out of them. I do not recommend using local satellites to coordinate the timing of the attacks. After all, you have just travelled from another galaxy light years away, you are entirely capable of sending a simple signal they cannot detect to a handful of your own vessels. Or fuck it, if you aren't capable of that, synchronize your wrist-watches with the fleet's captains during a fucking simple meeting. Remember, you want to create an overwhelming feeling of loss and hopelessness in the defenders. Their only concern should be running, staying alive and worrying about their loved ones. Then it's a simple matter of mopping up, destroying their communication arrays and publicly offing their politicians. Once their world goes silent you can move on, leaving your rear guard to exterminate or enslave the remaining survivors as you see fit. Also known as shock and awe.

14.2 Orbital Bombardment. Useful when the planet you're taking has strong ground forces. The first goal of any orbital bombardment is to take out any weapons capable of deep-space firing-solutions and aerial vehicles. After which you can pick apart ground forces, communication capabilities and civilians at your leisure.

14.3 Podding. When you do not enjoy a significantly more powerful force, there are a few options you can consider instead of invading. Covert body snatching or podding is a perfectly respectable option. If it isn't a natural genetic option, reach out to your science advisors for the appropriate technology. Essentially you want to send a few troops into rural locations around the globe where they can gradually infiltrate the residents, kidnapping, killing and assuming their identities. It's a slow process but very effective. Once you have strong outposts you can start reaching into smaller cities and assimilating them into the fold. Be careful to not reach too high too fast. Very often a naive fifth columnist will get cocky and attempt to take a president or congressman but that is unnecessary and dangerous. Slow and steady podding wins the day.

14.4 Coming in peace with secret, nefarious purposes may be a bit of a cliché but still a highly effective way of establishing a beach-head. You will be surprised how gullible and trusting some species can be. Coming in peace allows you to infiltrate and corrupt their politics, clergy and media houses, buying time while you go about feasting on them and readying yourself for the overt action which is the next stage. In some cases the ruse has lasted for centuries but I lack the patience for the long game. It's important to not look too terrifying to the locals, offer up petty technologies and cures to common ailments. Smile, kiss babies and try to avoid eating people who will be missed in the beginning.

14.5 Beat into submission. There will be times when the goal of an invasion is not the annihilation and dominance of the race but instead a desire to have them join your empire. Obviously the best way to show them the benefits of signing up is to beat them into submission, then, when they are defeated, sitting down and magnanimously inviting them to join in your glorious cause. If they agree, let them have the planet to themselves. I always like to keep a few officials around. That way, when they turn against you, your representatives will be killed and you will know it's time to reinvade.

14.6 Giant reptiles. Imagine this scenario. Picture a large bustling city… oh I don't know… let's say, Tokyo, for example, and imagine the millions of people bustling around, going about their circadian rhythms, when a giant shadow falls across large swathes of the city. People look up in horror, scream and start running in terror. Imagine a giant, bipedal reptile, coated in a viscous fluid, roaring so loud it shatters windows all across downtown, showering civilians and cars in shards of toughened 5mm plate glass. Now it starts to walk, this abomination, each step being measured by a seismograph a few miles out of town. This reptile rears up, smashing high-rise buildings and sending debris falling, trampling cars and tanks underfoot, unaware of their existence. Slow natives disappear beneath its massive claws with naught but the slightest squishing sounds emanating down the street. Now imagine, amidst all the sirens and gun fire and screaming, a small light on the horizon, slowly descending from the heavens off in the distant. Did you notice it? Would anyone? Nope. Nobody would. Now imagine that the light was, in fact, a vessel crammed with your crack troops landing at a predesignated coordinate. Giant marsupials, or anything similar, such as monsters, robots, flailing tentacle-beasts, all work just as well. The goal here is simply misdirection and it's a highly effective and fun invasion method. If you're wondering where you would get giant reptiles for such a purpose, you could simply take regular ones and rear them in a high oxygen and steroid environment, with some minor genetic modifications, or simply place them on an island and expose them to radiation. If your scientists can't do that, there's a lovely little moon on the seventh planet in the inner-most solar system of the Grixxon galaxy, that produces lizards and marsupials perfect for this purpose. Simply build the required space vessel and pick a few up at your leisure. Don't be greedy, leave enough for the next generation of warmongers.

14.7 Gloops, slimes, blobs and Nanotech are equally fun and effective if giant lizards are a bit too garish for your tastes. Any half decent scientist should be able to produce a good gloop in a matter of months. Insist that the gloop produced is immune to fire and projectile damage and preferably capable of devouring the flesh of the inhabitants without damaging the structures they inhabit. Just ensure you can control the slime when it's done its job. There have been occurrences where the gloop infested the entire planet making it inhospitable to the invaders themselves. It should always be vulnerable to one substance, frequency, or weapon you can use to kill it when its mission is at an end.

14.8 Psychic Takeover. If your species has a small population and some measure of psychic ability, this might be an option to you. The game play is the same as podding only you will be controlling inhabitants via psychic means instead of wearing their skins.

14.9 Farming. If you take out missile and air defenses of the planet, the game is already won. Generally it's a good idea to cut communication and eliminate the larger standing armies, just so the locals get the message but after that, feel free to kick back. There's no need to hurry, why not take what you need in the quantities you like and allow the planet to replenish itself. This way you can live off the planet while readying yourself for the next invasion. If there are minerals you want to mine, by all means wipe that continent clean of insurgents and their families. Otherwise, leave them alone and harvest them only when necessary; keep the planet in balance and your belly full.

14.10 Ruling the Masses. A Lazy option for invaders who want the resources of the planet but lack the manpower or the work ethic to do the digging themselves. Have your ships appear above their cities and then appear before their leader. During that meeting, express your desire for the resource using and give them a few days to prepare it and place it at a location of your choosing. If they fail to provide the meat, liquid or mineral as requested, kill a few million and then politely ask again. They will soon realize you aren't to be trifled with. Once they start providing, you can gradually increase the amount. It helps if you have a spaceship in geosynchronous orbit above you to issue instructions, perform miraculous eclipses on command or to set assassins on fire.

14.11 Kill 'em all. Sometimes it just isn't worth the effort. Sometimes you don't have the resources or soldiers to engage the enemy on the ground. Sometimes they taste like rubber and the only vegetation available is all lettuce and mushroom. Sometimes it just makes better sense to set fire to the outer surface of the planet and then leave it to cool down. Some people just like to watch a planet burn.

14.12 Decision tree on invasion types

Below is a decision tree to help you pick the invasion strategy that is best suited to your situation:

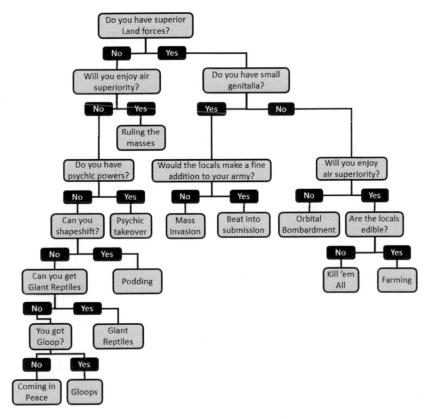

Figure 14. Decision Tree - Invasion types.

15 Space Combat – Vehicles

15.1 Basic control systems

Let's start by discussing what types of control systems are available to a modern warmonger such as yourself.

15.1.1 Auto vessels are those with navigational and piloting capabilities built into the very hardware of the craft itself. These systems use an array of proximity sensors which feed into a processing unit to determine the best course of action. You tell it where you want to go and it will get you there quickly and safely.

15.1.2 Bio-Piloted vessels are controlled by biological entities, some societies still believe biologicals have the ability to react quicker and more creatively than synthetic systems. The complicated navigational calculations are normally processed by software and the vectors are "suggested" to the meat in the seat via a console of some kind.

15.1.3 Robotic pilots. Identical in functionality to that of an auto vessel, the difference is that the computational and decision-making technology is housed within a mobile, stand-alone unit resembling a biological pilot. These units are usually protected by materials strong enough to protect the expensive inner workings of the robot. The advantage of a robotic pilot is, if a ship is destroyed, these sturdy pilots can be retrieved from the wreckage and assigned to another vessel. Also, when the field marshal realizes how incompetent his biologicals are at piloting, these can be brought on board any vessel without any engineering or retrofitting.

15.1.4 Fly by unwire. A cost effective solution which has all the calculations and piloting conducted at a remote site, only direct signals to engines and thrusters are sent to the vessel, which then reacts accordingly. The actual thinking, navigating and piloting takes place far away from the vessel itself, normally on a secret base buried on an obscure moon or on a central, defended vessel kept out of harm's way. Unwire technology allows for instantaneous communication between ship and remote pilot. It's important to note that while this is a cost-effective solution, the crews of such vessels tend to sleep uneasily knowing if the pilot fucks up, he might at worst receive reduced rations for a day before being assigned a new vessel, whereas the crew themselves will be out, floating in the abyss, with nothing to listen to but the hiss of their oxygen venting through a tear in their suit. A common solution is to place a placebo in a seat that looks and behaves like a robotic pilot, only, in truth, is little more than a reassuring chatterbot wearing a captain's hat.

15.1.5 Tethering. It's not always cost effective to provide drives and piloting systems to all of your space faring vessels. A popular solution to this is tethering. Similar to how humans tow away damaged vehicles. Robust cables are attached from the powered tugs to the gliders. The tug, when accelerating, pulls the gliders forward along with it. It's important to understand the dangers of slowing down, with negligible friction available in space, when your drive vessel reverses thrust, your gliders won't. The best solution is to simply use rigid tethers which function as both ties and struts.

15.2 Vehicular propulsion methods

5.2.1 Negative mass drives. An elegant solution based around the ultimate traffic enforcement officer of the universe, known only as 'c' to its citizens. This drive cleverly manipulates space, by constricting it in front of the vessel and expanding the space behind it, the vessel becomes capable of incredible speeds. The problem you will struggle with is locating the negative mass required but it's out there.

15.2.2 Magsails use large magnetic fields set up to catch solar winds which propel them. Very often these vessels are compared to sailing a small yacht on a pond, in a gentle breeze on a sunny afternoon. A more accurate analogy would be a hot air balloon over the cape of storms, with passengers in the flimsy basket screaming as they find themselves subjected to terrifying forces beyond their ken or influence. While such transporters are referred to as 'vessels' by salesmen, I personally prefer the nautical definition of 'planetary jetsam.'

15.2.3 The blood of our ancestors. This has to be my favorite aspect of Earthling culture. To take hydrocarbons, formed from the dead corpses of algae, zooplankton, dinosaurs and other ancient ancestors to propel your vehicles is the coolest method I have yet to witness anywhere, ever. Sure it's inefficient and will probably poison your planet but for style: full points. Kudos to your comeuppance celebration by burning your forefathers in your engines to take you places they couldn't even dream of. However, that being said, the power-to-weight ratio required to use hydrocarbons for space travel is entirely impractical.

15.2.4 Blinkers. In a parallel universe, the place you want to get to is only a few thousand yards from where you are right now. Regardless of where you want to be. Blinking technology will allow you to slip your vessels into that dimension, travel the short distance and re-appear in your universe at the designated spot. It's really that simple. The only complication is knowing which of the infinite parallel universes to use. There are some extra-dimensional species with an arcane understanding of the planes. Simply buy a copy of the Necronomicon and learn the required rituals to summon them. They will normally ask for a toll, a percentage of the souls transported. Feel free to negotiate and insist on the warmonger discount. Very often, if you agree on a round trip, they will only take the souls on the return trip, leaving you with a full fighting force for the invasion. More than fair.

15.2.5 Teleportation. In reality, teleportation makes copies of the scanned images and places the duplicates in the desired position. It doesn't transport the original. If your popular Earthling TV series was accurate, a Scottish gentlemen would walk out after every beaming, and shoot each unsuspecting member of the away-team in the head. They would then cut to a scene where Starfleet housekeeping is seen dragging the body of the captain away for incineration, while another follows behind, mopping up his blood. Aside from this one drawback, it also has massive energy demands.

15.2.6 Lazar drives. Bob Lazar is an Earthling scientist who discovered he was working on an extra-terrestrial propulsion system while employed by the US Military. He claimed the fuel employed was element 115 of the periodic table. At that time no such element existed, but anyone with the ability to count could have predicted it. He stated that a stable isotope for 115 was used by Reticulans for drives, which is of course ridiculous because Reticulans don't employ FTL technology. They believe FTL to be a heretical act, bypassing the wonders of the universe without witnessing its beauty. That being said, element 115 does provide an effective means by which to manipulate space/time to your advantage and will allow for faster than light travel. I suspect Slothons provided the technology. Slothons, of course, are shape shifters and might have taken Reticulan form which humans are accustomed to, to coerce them into fixing their vessel. Slothons are devious like that.

15.3 Basic Vessel types

15.3.1 Targets. Medium sized ships used to draw fire and protect bigger, better vessels. Normally with bulwark hulls and if manned, have crews consisting of suicidal, expendable, coffee-drinkers.

15.3.2 Scouts. Small, lightly armored vessels with your finest drives. Their goal is to look out for enemy units, identify signs of life and report back what they have learned.

15.3.3 Decoys. Large empty vessels designed to look like juicy targets but which in fact have only basic propulsion, often tethered when moving vast distances. Should have rudimentary weapons that look terrifying. Similar to targets.

15.3.4 Pods. When vessels are struck during combat, using bulkheads and compartmentalization systems, crew members, when informed of the impending life-support-system failure, can take a leisurely stroll to one of several life pods and jettison themselves to safety. Then, while enjoying a selection of music and beverages, they can patiently wait for a timeous rescue from nearby ships. That's the theory. In reality: A big explosion is heard and screaming ensues until all the air is drawn out into space, then silence descends while everybody dies an agonizing death. It is always thus. Don't waste your money on life-pods.

15.3.5 Weapon platforms. Medium sized vessels with top-end weaponry which will be used to engage in space conflict. Most of these are versatile and can be used within atmospheres to support ground invasions with orbital bombardment capabilities.

15.3.6 Fighters. Small, sleek and agile vessels designed to engage similar or larger vehicles. Their agility allows them to avoid being locked on while they fire at enemy vessels. They are the backbone of any defensive or offensive strategy. Good fighters will double as aircraft in planetary invasions.

15.3.7 Transporters. Massive carriers of troops and cargo, useful when transporting large forces needed for invasions, they should be well armored, as they will be the primary target in every skirmish unless, of course, you have a mother ship.

15.3.8 Mother ships. Normally a gargantuan vessel which houses fighters, officers and brothels. They can be the size of cities and will double as your home base and HQ while the invasion is underway. Normally the largest orbital bombardment weapons will be fitted to this ship. Defend it at all costs. Within the lower ranks of my navy this vessel was often referred to as 'mama' or 'your mama'. With many references being made regarding how big she was. Often the vessels exhaust ports and docking bays are spoken about. The lackey classes seemed to find these necessary features to be somehow humorous or worthy of ridicule.

15.3.9 Tender ships. These are small utility vessels, designed to service the fleet. Their purpose is to provide the required refueling, maintenance, waste extraction, atmospheric scrubbing or food distribution to the other vessels. In a pinch they can be used as decoys or target units to protect more important assets.

15.4. Illustration of Vessel types

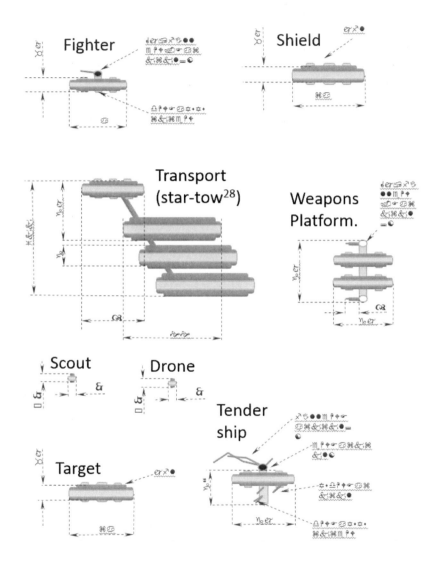

Figure 15. Vessel Types.

16. Space Combat – Tactics

Space is a funny place. It isn't a pure vacuum, not scientifically speaking. A captain of any space-going vessel will quickly learn to respect the abyss and her mysterious ways. Robotic captains even more so. In battle, they will have endless solutions about hyper-drives, flanking maneuvers and adjusting shield strengths. Pay no attention to them. They were hired to fly the vessels as you order them to.

Any fleet travelling out to meet an enemy's armada needs only two things to guarantee a win. You need ships capable of inflicting damage and ships you don't mind losing. If you have more ships you don't mind losing than they have vessels capable of inflicting damage, you will win. If you don't, you will lose.

So in this regard, space conflict is quite simple.

I urge you, when transporting troops and equipment for an invasion to do it surreptitiously. Your army is at its most vulnerable while in deep space. Whatever route you had planned while preparing should be altered at the last minute to prevent an ambush. Scouts and drones should always advance before your fleet and care should be taken to check moons, gas clouds and asteroids as these are prime locations for sneak attacks. At the final staging point, vessels should be scanned for explosives and alien saboteurs and only then should crew and cargo be admitted. All cargo being loaded onto the vessel should be scrutinized and passengers should be subjected to rigorous security processes, including but not limited to thorough strip searches.

The money you spend on space transport should be the biggest line-item of the entire invasion. Let it be so, don't compromise on this one, older or inferior vessels might save you money up front but you will pay with the lives of your soldiers and reduced invasion capabilities instead.

If the enemy has a larger force, lure them into separating into smaller units and destroy those one at a time. If they won't fall for that, consider their speeds, their maneuverability, their fire power, defense structures and the skill of their pilots compared to yours. Look for weaknesses you can capitalize on. Every armada has inherent vulnerabilities you will be able to adapt your tactics to take advantage of.

If you've read any space-warfare literature you will find full chapters dealing with formations. There is no need to memorize the horns of the Nebraxian butterfly or the intricate attack patterns of Forleithian hunting swallows to become an effective air commander. Instead, my advice would be to keep it simple. Pick an angle where they have the worst firing solution directed on you and where you can return fire at a greater rate than them. If they attack you, enter into a strategic retreat, drawing in the enemy while you run simulations to find the best solution, once you have it calculated, dispatch the orders to all your units and execute.

If they have poor sensors, mount stealth attacks with boarding parties to take control or destroy their vessel from the inside. If they are slower then you, don't show it, draw them into following you and then leave them stranded light years away, while you take their planet in their absence. If they have superior fire power, concentrate all your attacks on those weapons first and ensure everything they shoot at is expendable by throwing vessels and captains you don't like in front of those you do.

If your weapons enjoy better range, stay back and snipe them out of existence. If you are more maneuverable, simply move in amongst them, this will prevent them from shooting without risking damaging their own vessels.

In short, don't be where they expect you to be. Do what they wouldn't have thought possible or sensible. Identify their weaknesses and exploit them. If they will destroy something of yours, make sure it is of your choosing and not theirs. In this way you can make a superior army insignificant. Long range tactical nukes are always an option too. For more information on space tactics review the sections on surface tactics and subterfuge, the principles are identical but for the third dimension.

17. Modern Ground Weaponry and Vehicles

I am not able to describe all the different types of weaponry available in the known universe, it just can't be done. For every tribe of every sentient creature on every inhabited planet, each have their own special weapons. Some are as unique as the cultures from which they were created and their abilities to kill and maim range from mild bruising to planet-wide decimation. From small hand-held devices to ships with their own gravities, the variation on weapons is as infinite in complexity as the stars. That is not my intention here, what you, as an aspiring commander in chief, need to know is how to classify weapons and name them appropriately to prevent being mocked by generals, arms traders and sergeants in your own army.

17.1 Small arms are any weapons which you can pick up and hand to a soldier before sending him out to kill with it. They are as varied as the faces of my victims I see at night, but if used correctly they can sway any war in your favour.

17.1.1 Primitive melee weapons are any which can be used in melee combat, this includes natural attacks such as tentacles, claws, prehensile genitalia or manufactured weapons like clubs, swords, whips, axes and anything similar. Primitive civilizations use these weapons on a daily basis and one should never under-estimate how effective they can be in a melee situation. Best to shoot their wielders from a distance, and quickly, instead of letting them get close enough to show you how they work. In human history, there are several examples of how rifle wielding infantry have been cut down by motivated spear-wielding warriors. The finest example of this being the battle of Isandlwana in Kwa-Zulu Natal. The Zulu melee weapon of choice was called the 'Iklwa' so named because that's the sound it makes when you pull it out of someone's guts, which is, obviously, fucking poetry.

17.1.2 Monofilament melee devices are bladed melee weapons with a powered edge, making use of modern monoblade technology. I will leave the science aside as its quite complex but think of it as a very, very sharp blade that can cut through carbon fiber, diamond and steel like a watery chicken broth. I would advise against equipping any of your infantry with monofilament blades, as the death rates and amputations in training far exceed any battlefield kills and dismemberments they will inflict. There is now a monofilament whip and three-sectioned staff available. The only plausible application I could see with these would be to drop them in the enemy camp and let them cut off their own dangly bits while trying to figure out how they work.

17.1.3 Chain weapons. Swords, axes, polearms. Not much more impressive than the device your father used to cut down trees when you were a whelp. Regardless of how terrifying they look in horror movies they are ridiculous, unwieldy weapons. Only effective if you are fighting slow undead or stationary fungal warriors.

17.1.4 Light. Swords, sabers and staffs come in various colors and sizes. Unfortunately these are as lethal as day-old kittens because light just isn't weaponizable like that. That being said, these devices make for fantastic torches and safe, fun toys for children.

17.1.5 Power weapons. Very similar to chain weapons but equipped with smaller motors, sharper blades and finer designs. These can be considered effective close-combat items but only after ten years of intensive training on an isolated mountaintop, under the close scrutiny of an old man with semi-mystical powers.

17.2 Ranged Weapons. If an attack can be made from a distance it's called a ranged weapon. Again, primitives have been cleverly throwing and propelling wood, stone and metals at one another with deadly results for millennia. Nowadays modern ranged weapons come in a few forms:

17.2.1 Pistols – Normally small weapons which can be held in one hand, tentacle or claw.

17.2.2 Compact Combat guns – Sometimes called submachine guns. These generally offer higher rates of fire than pistols and suit short-range urban-combat settings.

17.2.3 Blasters. Any weapons which fire multiple projectiles in one shot. A shotgun is a good example.

17.2.4 Assault rifles. The standard-issue weapon for infantry. Generally compact rifles with quick reloading clips and medium length barrels. Most have a variable rate of fire, single shots and bursts. Some have full-automatic settings, which is more effective in movies than actual combat situations.

17.2.5 Sniper rifles. Similar to assault rifles but with longer barrels and better sighting systems to allow for a more accurate shot. They are designed to offer the best range of any small arms types. They generally have a low fire-rate.

17.2.6 Light machine guns. This is a misnomer, you wouldn't call one of these light if you had to lug it for three days on a heavy gravity moon for training purposes. Light machine guns are heavy, rapid-firing rifles, very often equipped with a tripod or mounted to a hard-point of a vehicle or bunker. Offer a high rate of fire and large magazine capacity. Although this is getting close to violating the definition of small arms, in many cases an LMG can be disassembled and transported in pieces by a fire team instead of one soldier.

17.3 Ammunition / Power systems. Let's have a quick look into what types of ammunition and power systems are available to you. It's important to understand not only the lethality of the chosen power type but the reliability of the weapons, the cost, rate of fire and the environmental influence of each weapon type. Whichever is selected, all your soldiers should be well trained in that weapon in a similar environment to the combat arena.

17.3.1 Death rays are a common choice, this is patented technology so what exactly goes into a 'death ray' is open to speculation, although the consistent lethal results are not. Due to its slow rate of fire they come in only two flavors: Pistols and sniper rifles.

17.3.2 Projectile and Bolter weapons fire solid slugs of metal or ceramics at a high velocity. The mechanical energy when impacting on the target can puncture flesh and lead to quick or slow deaths, depending on the caliber, range and initial velocity of the round.

17.3.3 Phasers. These are ridiculous weapons and about as lethal as introducing low levels of aspartame into the drinking supply of your enemy. At best, phasers might stun a small mammal for a few minutes, if it has congenital heart problems. Issue these only to security guards defending facilities you don't care about and to kindergarten teachers for disciplinary purposes.

17.3.4 Arc technology fires an electric arc of an immense voltage and amperage; though the nature of electricity makes this less accurate than other weapon types. The results speak for themselves, arcing has the advantage of being able to negate most powered armor suits and if a direct hit is made, causes super-heating of internal bodily fluids. If your enemy is edible, think of it as killing and broiling at the same time. Like jam tarts and snackwiches, be careful to let them cool down a bit before eating. Never let the beams of arc rifles cross as it can result in an explosion of significant proportions. Also effective against ethereal and psychic-based entities.

17.3.5 Laser. Perhaps the most popular weapon type and with good reason. It is an efficient and simple technology that's easy to maintain. Equip lasers with portable solar or fission power generators and you won't have to worry about ammunition for the duration of the campaign. The only drawback is the silly sound they make when firing and their inability to instill fear in the enemy.

17.3.6 Plasma. In my opinion, plasma technology does not lend itself to pistols. The devices tend to be bulky and unreliable. Even the best on the market offer only a few shots before the batteries are drained and you're standing with an expensive weapon consisting of too much plastic to effectively substitute as a club. Plasma is the perfect medium for fantastic sniper rifles. If your species is strong or robotic, purchase plasma assault rifles with extra battery packs and they become fantastic weapons.

17.3.7 Gamma rays. Small, light and handy devices, they are easy to conceal and lethal when wielded by trained experts. The gamma ray is a fine medium as it isn't noticeably influenced by weather, atmosphere or gravity. Unfortunately these can also be extremely expensive. To issue these to all your troops will more than likely bankrupt you. I personally only hand them out to senior officers and female spies I intend on shtüping in the near future.

17.4 Artillery Systems. Artillery is a classification of weaponry effective well beyond the range of small arms. Due to the nature of the ammunition and range, artillery if often referred to as indirect fire. Your Emperor Napoleon once said that God favors the nation with the best artillery and he has yet to be proven wrong.

17.4.1 Mortars are perhaps the simplest devices on a modern battlefield but they remain highly effective and portable indirect fire systems. It's essentially a tube placed on a base plate, the mortar itself holds all the working bits. The angle between the tube and plate can be adjusted to allow for aiming. The trick to using a mortar accurately is to have a basic understanding of geometry, parabolas, gravity, wind, atmospheric pressure, drag, chemistry and Newtonian physics. A little psychic intuition to know where the enemy will be in five seconds time is handy too. Weights, sizes and gauges vary greatly. Tip: Make it mobile. Put it on the back of a truck. Use delayed launchers with disposable mortar units to reduce the risk of being caught when you're the insurgency.

17.4.2 Land Artillery. Large guns firing heavy-gage rounds, most modern land artillery is mechanized and these combat vehicles are armored to protect the systems and personnel. However, do not confuse mobile artillery with tanks, as their purpose on the battlefield is entirely different. Basic artillery fires rounds from five hundred meters to ten kilometers away. The advanced systems can stretch well beyond that. Very often the rounds are adjusted by a spotter unit with eyes on the target.

17.4.3 Disposable Drones. Aerial, unmanned vehicles designed to carry a payload to a specific point and then detonate or disperse. Relatively cheap and more accurate than other dispersal systems.

17.4.4 Ocean Artillery is only likely to be used in planetary defense. Large guns firing massive rounds with a good range but a lousy accuracy. If they are hitting with any accuracy the enemy is adjusting their firing solution using spotters, drones or satellites. Jam all communications and they will be blind.

17.4.5 Rocket propelled grenade launchers are shoulder-mounted weapons which fire small rockets at distances far greater than rifles. They can prove extremely useful on many occasions. Though notoriously inaccurate, newer models have automated targeting systems.

17.4.6 Grenade launcher. Sometimes attached to the underside of an assault rifle, these fire grenades a shorter distance than an RPG but still further than throwing them. They make an amusing 'thunk' sound when fired.

17.4.7 Orbital Artillery. The go-to solution for any problem a planet can muster. If you drop a titanium rod, just a simple metal staff, from ten thousand meters, the impact will leave a crater deep enough to bury a tank in. Imagine how much worse the impact would be if the rod had an HE core. If you've brought enough ammunition with you, you can annihilate a planet but if you're planning on invading afterwards, orbital artillery can be used to soften up strong-holds, scatter force build-ups or destroy tanks, bases and cities as you require.

17.4.8 Missiles are equally capable of long-distance, devastating bombardments. Artillery rounds are fired by a propellant out of a gun, after which it is subject to natural forces to determine where it lands. Missiles accelerate for a longer period of time, using propellant housed within the projectile itself. Most modern missiles are capable of adjusting their trajectory whilst in flight, allowing for a more accurate weapon. They're also much more expensive. In military terms, a rocket is a small arms weapon, while missiles are launched from a ship, vehicle, structure or spaceship.

Now we have discussed some of the means of dispensing indirect fire, we need to discuss the actual payloads themselves. They vary from planet to planet but I have selected a few here which are more common, also items which might give you an idea or two:

17.5 Artillery Payloads

17.5.1 Chemical rounds. Any acrid or poisonous gas or powder of your choosing, preferably one which will cause armor to corrode, lungs to clog, skin to melt or intestines to explode.

17.5.2 Napalm. Think of napalm as petroleum in a gel state. It burns at a slower rate and sticks to flesh and armor like external testicles in cold weather. It's also a very popular scent amongst generals.

17.5.3 High explosive (HE) Effective against armor, groups of infantry, buildings, vehicles, headquarters, latrines, yoga classes, nurseries and pensioner warehouses.

17.5.4 Tactical nukes. Even more effective than HE rounds. They have a range of about a kilometer, with a very high mortality rate. The drawback to this weapon type is, you will be unable to view and gloat over the dead without radioactive protection or ten years of patient waiting.

17.5.5 Smokers. These are non-lethal rounds which reduce visibility. Handy for a retreat or to provide soft cover for your advancing troops. Be careful with smoke as it leaves both sides blind.

17.5.6 Flare rounds. These provide a lofty light source with which to do battle beneath. Some have parachutes, wings, or propellers attached to keep the device hanging longer.

17.5.7 Psychic rounds. These explode above the ground and release a resonating pulse which can disrupt mental processes for a short period of time, depending on the power setting, the natural cerebral shielding of the enemy, and the durability of their nervous systems.

17.5.8 Intelligent gloop rounds explode above the surface to spray an area of around ten meters in a gloop of your choosing. Sentient gloops will quickly regroup and advance on the nearest living creatures, forcing defenders to turn their attention from the perimeter, to the screams of the REMFs behind them. At which time you can approach the location at your leisure.

17.5.9 Nanites – similar to gloops only less messy, uses tiny robots instead of bio-based substances. Nanites are easier to program to attack a specific uniform, species, race, or individual of your choosing.

17.5.10 Robot rounds. If you have robots that can assemble themselves, fire them behind enemy lines and let them do their stuff. You can high five them when you meet over the corpses of your fallen foe.

17.5.11 Sticky gloop rounds. Non-intelligent gloop explodes above the surface and coats the ground with an industrial-strength gel adhesive. Taking a few seconds to harden, it reduces the abilities of soldiers to fight, run or reload their weapons. So much fun.

17.5.12 Microbial rounds. If your scientists have devised any microbe, virus, bacteria or fungus which could wreak havoc on the health of others, feel free to have it loaded and placed into microbial dispersal rounds.

17.5.13 Little horrors / hatchlings. Most planets have some nasty insectoids that can burrow into people's intestines, taking the awkward route before beginning to feast; Flies that lay their eggs in eyeballs; Wigs that work their ways into brains or mosquito's with acidic venom. Anything small and terrifying, take 'em, freeze 'em and place them into canisters and fire at the enemy.

17.5.14 Honey rounds. Think of the meanest, toughest animal, no bigger than a dog, on your planet. For Earth – consider the honey badger. Imagine if the honey badger had two desires: One – to eat honey, and, two – to kill anything trying to eat its honey. Imagine if you could harness that aggression to fight on the side of good? Now you can. With lab-bred honey badgers caged and waiting for deployment, simply fire a couple of these honey rounds into the ranks of the enemy and then open the cages. Watch the hilarity unfold, set to a soundtrack of pleas and screaming from the enemy while being eaten and torn apart. Be careful your animal rights activists don't find out about this mode of attack or they will be lobbying and bombing your duma. Truth of the matter, it's not cruel at all, the honey badger doesn't care about silly things like freedom and laboratory experiments. Don't bother troding them either, it just pisses them off further.

17.5.15 EMP round. These are high altitude devices which, when fired properly can shut down electronic equipment. Historically this effect was created by triggering a nuclear explosion above the ionosphere and letting the ions do the work. Now the EMP can be localized and the effect tailored to suit your required range.

17.6 Unique Items

17.6.1 Lightning rods. This is an interesting weapon system consisting of several components, which I first witnessed in the hands of the enemy, using it to devastating effect. Instead of firing lightning, by targeting a victim with the rifle you designate it to be struck from above, by the super-charged atmosphere you previously created.

17.6.2 Brain-resonating audio systems. Terrifying weapon systems consisting of custom-built audio projection devices, which cause physical vibrations of brains, jellies and jams within earshot. If powerful enough, the resonations will lead to a brain exploding. Get your scientists to look into standing waves and the required frequencies for enemy brain-masses. Only if they are sufficiently dissimilar to your own soldiers should this weapon be considered. If you use this device within a facility you intend on occupying, you're going to need a squad of housekeepers with strong stomachs to clean up all the grey or green brain juice.

17.6.3 Fulgurator. An explosive which detonates using a paint-then-trigger system. Fantastic for tactical withdrawals and for barbeques in base camps after victories.

17.6.4 Auto turrets. Simple, static, stand-alone systems set up to look for movement and shoot it. Great for defensive and anti-flanking.

17.6.5 Landmines. Primitive robotic explosive devices, specializing in maiming and killing. Their only tactic is to hide under a tuft of dirt and wait. They are extremely patient, some have waited for centuries before jumping out and yelling surprise in their own special way. Some specialize in vehicles and others in infantry and grazing beasts.

17.6.6 IEDs. Think of these as a poor man's landmine but never underestimate their potency and ingenuity to look like any other wonderful thing worthy of your attention. Equally patient and often more deadly than landmines.

17.7 Aerial Vehicles

17.7.1 Bombers. Large aerial vehicles designed to drop payloads with precision.

17.7.2 Fighters. Small agile vehicles used to engage in air combat, taking out enemy bombers, fighters, or copters. Some have limited bombing or strafing capabilities.

17.7.3 Missile systems. Small aerial vehicles equipped with long range sensors and weaponry. Built to act similarly to auto-turrets.

17.7.4 Choppers. Aerial vehicles with vertical take-off and landing capabilities. Used for transporting troops, and supplies to front lines.

17.7.5 Gun ships are helicopters with powerful weapon systems. Limited transporting capabilities.

17.7.6 Drones. Unmanned aerial vehicles. If you place a synthetic pilot in the seat of a manned fighter jet, is it a drone? I don't fucking know.

17.8 Land Vehicles

17.8.1 'Squitos – insect sized robots, not nanites, with swarm capabilities. Each one loaded with a small needle, capable of introducing the victim to some nasty virus, toxin or fungus.

17.8.2 Blood hounds. Small, land-based, four-legged robotic units, designed to track, scout and secure perimeters. Often loaded with small explosive packs, allowing them to double as automated jihadists when needed.

17.8.3 Big dogs. Similar to blood hounds but capable of carrying light loads, normally additional ammunition and medical equipment.

17.8.4 Mules. Large robotic units capable of carrying heavy loads through difficult terrain. The new models are silent and allow them to move with a patrol or squad. Their primary role is to extract wounded soldiers and take them to the nearest triage tent.

17.8.5 Tanks are heavily armored vehicles used in front-line fighting. They are propelled with tracks, anti-grav, or hovertech and are highly mobile weapons platforms. Small fusion or fission reactors are preferable to diesel units as tanks have massive energy requirements. Ensure all your tanks have good communication and brewing facilities on board. Also, insist on a hole in the floor, nothing big, the size of a large bathplug will suffice and will help when crews are liquefied, cooked or nanited and the tank needs to be hosed-down before being reissued. The hole will also help with day-to-day ablutions. Male tanks are equipped with large caliber cannons or missile turrets used in front line fighting. Female tanks are equipped with anti-personnel weapons including LMGs, Mortars, Flamethrowers and lightning systems.

17.8.6 Mechs are heavily armed vehicles built to take advantage of bipedal movement. This allows them to move with an agility not afforded to tracked or hoverteched vehicles. They tend to be prime targets for enemy attacks and as such work as focus elements. Best to place soldiers who are bright enough to operate heavy machinery but not much more than that. They look great in parades and on the cover of Death Weekly.

17.8.7 APCs are armored personnel carriers, trucks used to lug grunts from one section of hell to another. Some are tracked, half tracked, hovertech or anti-grav units but most often these are wheeled. Sometimes fitted with LMGs or other similar weapon systems. The shape of the chassis and base tend to be angular to allow for landmine blasts to be deflected away from the vehicle.

17.8.8 Bakkies. Makeshift military vehicles, normally a pickup truck with mounted LMGs on the load-body. Surprisingly cheap and effective, a very popular option for your more budget-conscious warmonger for backwater shitholes everywhere. They can also double as a poor man's APC, though there generally isn't much A to the PC.

17.8.9 Alien mounts are often available on rural planets. They are cheap and trainable units with readily-available fuel. If your troops can master them, feel free to use them. Some species travel with their mounts from one planet to another but the chances of them being useful in another environment is unlikely and the logistics costs are ridiculous. If they can fly, even better. If caught out in a blizzard, they can also double as tents and sleeping bags. Apparently.

17.8.10 Alien attack beasts. When invading planet after planet, you might stumble across a few creatures you come to appreciate for their stalking and killing skills. By all means, let your scientists go to work with training and modifying these to suit integration into your army.

17.9 Shields and Armor

17.9.1 Natural armor. Thick hide, carapaces, shells, external skeletons, if your species naturally have any of these, congratulations, if not, why not start mucking about with inter-species gene splicing and develop a tough hide for your soldiers. Sure they will gripe about looking silly but they will thank you when it saves their lives on a battlefield. If mutating your subjects is beyond your science, why not grow skin separately and then surgically graft it to them?

17.9.2 Synthetic armor. This encompasses all primitive sorts of unpowered armor that people have been using since the first Neanderthal first put on an extra fur coat before going to war. It normally consists of metals, carbon-fiber, spider-silk, or similar materials which will do absolutely nothing when a gamma ray hits the chest. It's an effective way of reducing deaths and increasing the number of wounded and maimed. Why any general thinks this is beneficial is beyond me. It's also normally cumbersome stuff, slowing down the speed of infantry, tiring them sooner than necessary and costs more than blessed camo-spandex which is my recommended armor of choice.

17.9.3 Powered armor. Powered armor is something else entirely. The power is normally stored in deep-cycle, crystal batteries. The armor can weigh up to four hundred kilograms but it's an irrelevant number because powered armor will allow you to take that weight and more as if it was nothing. Good powered armor will allow a trooper to move faster, jump higher, and react quicker than regular unpowered warfighters. Powered armor will also offer effective protection against an array of weapons. Best is to identify what you're likely to be shot with and have the techs build in modules to defend against those systems. Some powered armor comes equipped with jetpacks to up the cool factor.

17.10 Image of popular small arms

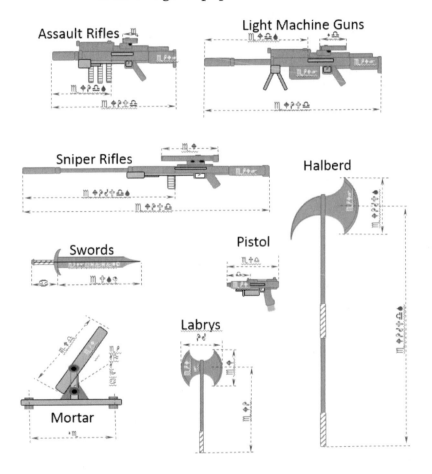

17.9.4 Force-field. There is no such thing. With regards to not getting shot, only the age-old options remain: shoot them first, duck, dodge, wear powered armor, or don't complain when you're bleeding out on a cold street.

17.9.5 Blessed spandex. It doesn't have to be spandex, any material capable of stretching will do. It offers almost no resistance or defense against any weapon types. The reason I issued this as my armor of choice was because it's light, cheap and allows the skin to breath. It also looks fantastic on female conscripts. I would have priests bless the spandex because soldiers believe in that sort of thing and that helps them when charging fortified positions.

18. Surface Conflict – Tactics

18.1 History and overview. A lot of people think the terms 'strategy' and 'tactics' are interchangeable. They aren't. Others believe one is a mental matter and the other physical. That is a dumbing down of the subtleties involved. I personally prefer this analogy: If your army was a single, giant, city-destroying monster, your tactics would be its nervous system, base brain functions and muscle memory, while its strategy would be how it intends eating all the Japanese people it can find, knocking down all of downtown Tokyo before moving on to Nagasaki to unleash more of the same.

Tactics are essentially how soldiers execute orders, while strategy is why, how and when you give out those orders. If that doesn't make sense, read it again and slowly. If it still doesn't compute, learn the words like a parrot so you can repeat them verbatim if you're ever asked.

Tactics are the result of training, drilling and standardized maneuvers you have entrenched into the minds of your warfighters; or the sub-routines scripted by field programmers uploaded to your synthetic-fighting-unit's CPUs.

18.2 Squad tactics

18.2.1 Run and gun. An effective means to close in on an enemy unit. One squad breaks cover, runs at a target, while a second squads shoots at the target. Once the first squad is in position, they provide cover fire for the second squad and so on. On paper it's a brilliant idea. In reality you're still running at a defended position, hoping to keep your guts off the battlefield.

18.2.2 Ambush. Ask any battle-hardened sergeant what his idea of a perfect date would be and he'll tell you it's an ambush. If you identify an area that's well trafficked by enemy troops, or a spot they're likely to traverse soon, you can prepare in advance for their coming. Terrain plays an important part in any ambush. The idea is to lure them into a predesignated kill-zone, where you have surprise and defensive positioning on your side. Landmines, mortars, artillery, snipers and grunts will be on stand-by, waiting for their units to reach a set point at which all hell breaks loose and everyone in the kill zone either:

    A. Dies
    B. Wants to

18.2.3 Counter ambush. A fictitious, ambitious piece of fluff, similar to contingency plans. It used to be known as 'run like fuck' but for purposes of moral was renamed, to imply being caught in a kill zone is unfortunate but can be overcome with team work, clear heads and accurate return-fire. Obviously that isn't the case.

18.2.4 Dig in. Any situation where your troops will be better positioned a few meters lower than the surface of the terrain. This will help for defensive purposes, making yourselves smaller targets and providing a degree of comfort for mole-people, hole-people and snake-based soldiery.

18.2.5 Target my position. Tactical murder/suicide, employing friendly artillery to act in the role of Doctor Kevorkian. Like playing Russian roulette with a loaded, cocked one-upped pistol.

18.2.6 Danger close. Tactical suicide employing friendly artillery to play the role of Doctor Kevorkian, with a slight chance of being paid out on your life insurance. Like playing Russian roulette with a partially, randomly loaded revolver.

18.2.7 Basic drills. These are simple things everyone does every day, only turned into a clear and concise process to ensure everyone does it the same way, which allows for more efficient teamwork. For example, how a squad should exit a vehicle when deploying. What soldiers should scream while on fire, bleeding or breathing chlorine. How to return sniper fire, execute a boskak (combat bowel movement), clear an enemy minefield or call in an artillery round. All of these are basic drills practiced time and again during basic training.

18.2.8 Pincer movement. An effective attack if executed quickly. It requires two separate forces attacking an enemy unit or column from opposite sides, preferably simultaneously. If successful you can split the force in twain. If unsuccessful, the movement will serve as a warning on the dangers of cross-fire.

18.2.9 Patrols. Nothing calms and centers a person like taking a brisk walk in the afternoon. There are many health benefits associated with keeping active and your troops will certainly appreciate the opportunity. Try to vary patrol sizes, times and routes as enemy miscreants might take advantage of these strolls to lay ambushes.

18.2.10 Suppressive fire. This is when soldiers shoot at something or someone and miss. Instead of admitting their failure they will use the term 'suppressive fire' claiming it somehow magically provides cover to friends or such nonsense. Do not tolerate this sort of blatant waste of ammunition.

18.2.11 Outrange. If your weaponry has a better range than the enemy's, it makes sense to keep your forces at a distance which allows you to remain lethal without giving your foe the same chance. If they advance, retreat the same distance while firing at them. If they retreat, advance to keep pace with them.

18.2.12 Feint Attack. A feint attack is a deliberate action designed to deceive the enemy into believing an attack is imminent, while in fact the attack will not take place as he perceives it. Sometimes feints are used as a distraction to lure units to counter the perceived threat, while you attack elsewhere or not at all.

18.2.13 Feint Retreat. Equally effective. By convincing the enemy you are retreating or about to, you can lure them into entering a potential ambush zone or leave them unprepared for counter strike.

18.2.14 Flank. A flanking maneuver is an attack on the sides of an enemy unit.

18.2.15 Outflank is the term used to describe the force you successfully performed the flanking maneuver on. That is, those too lazy to bother turning ninety degrees.

18.2.16 Charge. Also known as 'down the middle with smoke' this is perhaps the oldest of tactics. This highly intricate technique involves standing up, running at the enemy and screaming something.

18.2.17 Retreat. This is a tune my buglers were never taught. Of course, I learnt it in my academy days and if you are interested in how it sounds, they play something similar at the start of French rugby matches.
Whenever I found my forces being decimated, my generals would sometimes engage in reverse charges, pre-emptive withdrawals or strategic regroupings, but never retreats.

18.2.18 Dead Ground. Soldiers don't like to die. Sure, soldiers don't like to do a lot of things you make them do, but dying, even more so. They will try their utmost to prevent it from happening and you can use this fact to your advantage. When low on numbers, place your men without any means of escape and they will count as a superior force. Troding can have this effect for short amounts of time. Issue an order that any retreating will result in their executions and they will fight gallantly. If you try to use that order indefinitely during a protracted campaign, its efficacy will wane over time. Eventually troopers grow accustomed to their certain death and choose to accept it as inevitable.

18.2.19 High ground. Terrain with an elevated position can be advantageous for defending and sniping purposes. Try to hold the high ground wherever possible during a conventional war.

18.2.20 Mountainous terrain. Gives the advantages of high ground with the added benefit of physical obstacles and choke points, which will force any attackers to slow down and throw numbers at the problem when attempting to take this kind of terrain.

18.2.21 Recreational positioning. If you sit at the river long enough, downstream from the base or city you're napalming, you will see the crispy bodies of your enemies flow by. This is a favorite pastime of mine and Confucius. Try to get there before the bombardment starts with a few like-minded people. It helps to build the excitement if you make bets on the number of floaters.

18.2.22 Havoc. Most people believe havoc means chaos and destruction and sure, it's all that but it was also an order type. During medieval times, after a protracted siege a commander would call havoc when the wall finally came down and the invading army's soldiers were allowed to rape and pillage the inhabitants of the city with impunity. This was usually as a punishment for the city not surrendering and sieges being painful and dangerous undertakings by the invading armies. When Shakespeare said "Cry havoc and let slip the dogs of war" he was talking about this sort of order.

18.2.23. On courage. When I first read Sun Tzu I found it to be most insightful. I enjoyed his no-nonsense approach and clear, unfettered thinking. Then I came across a line which stated, quite matter-of-factly, that courage and cowardice is a matter of momentum. This frustrated me.

Stating that something as complex as courage could be addressed in such a simple statement infuriated me for quite some time. Eventually I flew to China and spent a few days learning Tangut. My days I spent in the local library and at night I would break into the Yinqueshan Han Tombs to study the original texts. It wasn't a translation problem. He really meant it. He really believed courage was as simple as a matter of momentum.

I was angry until I considered the words and realized he was entirely right.

Courage and cowardice is indeed a matter of momentum. In your personal life, in battle formations, in childhood development, momentum is the key to courage. And courage has the ability to confound and surprise even the most jaded of people.

In a classic battle you see it time and again. Your front line fighters clash with theirs, the killing commences. One person turns to flee and the moment everyone sees him run, it seems like a great idea to everyone. Within seconds your whole army is routing.

Training is the solution, where the soldier is exposed to horrible conditions and instructed to do incredibly dangerous and painful things. After a while they begin to believe they are capable of incredible feats and this contributes to the momentum and courage of the individual and the platoon.

Take a class at school. Any class, single out one child that is average and tell him he is brilliant and gifted at the subject. Watch what happens in a few years' time, very often that child will indeed fulfil the statement made, when it wasn't really accurate.

Your crack troops attack a standing army that is well dug in. One man charges a battery; runs straight into certain death and lobs a grenade. He's just set the standard. Watch as man after man, inspired by the first hero's contribution, takes on a seemingly invincible opponent and together, watch them surprise you, themselves and the enemy too as they tear into the well defended position. This is the true benefit of well-placed plants.

Courage and cowardice is indeed a matter of momentum. This is a simple and profound truth and if you learn how to master it, you have learned how to turn on courage in your troops and cowardice in everyone else's.

18.3 Grouping. If you haven't studied military history it can be confusing when you hear your subordinates reporting on events. For example, if one sergeant came into your office and said that three squads were killed in an ambush that morning and another told you that a division had been crippled with fungal crotch rot. Which is worse?

Well, you need to understand the basic grouping of military structures. Your generals will try to complicate the crap out of it, so I urge you to remind them that you're in charge and this is what each term means:

A Fire-team is the smallest group you can issue an order to. Normally two people. It's the minimal number of people capable of executing the simplest tactic – Run and Gun.

A Squad is made up of six fire-teams. You might want to mix up the weaponry within a squad and have one or two fire-teams carry something exotic, like a honey mortar or ray-gun-sniping system.

A Platoon consists of four squads.

A **Company** comprises of 4 platoons.

A **Battalion** is made up of four companies.

A **Regiment** includes two or more battalions. You can think of a regiment as a stand-alone army. If you placed a regiment on its own, in theory it should be capable of its own logistics, planning, support and theoretically even recruitment. There are historical reasons behind this and though I personally wouldn't recommend isolating them, you can think of them as a self-contained fighting force.

A **Brigade** consists of two regiments.

A **Division** is made of two brigades.

A **Corps** is comprised of two divisions.

Formation. Think of a formation as a working group, picked from all available forces on the board, to create a group capable of waging the war you intend to and placed under the control of one commander. There should be no confusion around who is in charge of every person, robot, vehicle and aircraft assigned to a formation. All regimental, company and speciality command lines, established during training or previous conflicts, need to be severed while those units are part of a formation. One commander is in charge and ultimately accountable for the formation. He is the person to shoot if things go wrong.

Army. Everyone. Some empires like to break their forces into several armies and give names to those. I find no value in this except when you have different species from separate planets. Multiple species don't always mix well, one always tends to eat the other. And communication issues can be troublesome.

Adding Up. While one brigade might equal two regiments, and each regiment consists of four battalions, one brigade does not equal eight battalions. It is never as simple as that. Remember, at every level, there are REMFs, officers, support units, chefs, scouts and others attached to certain designated groups. Also, within each division, there is comradery, history and pride associated within squads and regiments and these are an essential part of military life. Try not to fuck with it too much. Leave it to the generals to do that.

While we are covering military basics, below please find a table with the breakdown of military ranks and insignia, you need to commit it to memory:

18.4 Military Ranks and insignia

General

Lieutenant General

Major General

Brigadier General

Colonel

Lieutenant Colonel

Major

Captain

Lieutenant

2nd Lieutenant

Sergeant

Corporal

Lance Corporal

Private

19. Consolidating your Victory

If your invasion went according to plan, or if you improvised a win at a great cost, it's now irrelevant because you have the planet. Whether your new planet is a gem filled with wondrous natural beauties and exotic creatures or just another rock primed to be strip-mined, you should celebrate the victory.

Why waste the resources you ask? Well for motivational reasons mostly. Celebrating helps to cement your reign, allows you to brag about your victory and perhaps use it as an excuse to get that information officer you've had your eye on into a cocktail dress, then, if you play your cards right, out of it again.

If you chose to keep the invaded planet's species alive as allies, now would be a good time to get to know a bit about them. After all, all you learned about them up until now was how to kill them efficiently. If not, and the locals are edible, be sure to ship samples of the new meat to all your colonies throughout the empire and allow the people to enjoy the fruits of their labor.

It's important to make the citizenry believe they are somehow victors themselves. It helps to praise hardworking industrial workers, soldiers, teachers and mine workers. It's a nice way to unite groups of people who would otherwise despise each other.

19.1 Government. Refer to chapter three regarding the options open to you. It is critical you establish a strong government quickly because any planet left alone will develop a unique culture and identity. It's a matter of time before they start to consider independence as being an inalienable right. I tend to pick a general from my ranks and demote him or her to the role of planetary governor. Sure they'll be angry and take it out on the population but a firm hand is important.

19.2 Doomsday book. When William the Conqueror took

England, he commissioned a survey of his new kingdom. In the report, it detailed all the people, lands, animals and wealth of the nation and I would recommend you do the same, obviously just in a lot more detail. You should have the wealth, health and status of every citizen documented, along with the attractiveness of females and robustness of males. Weaponry, fuel, food stores, farms, vehicles and buildings should all be documented along with their previous owners. Full geological surveys should be executed, across the surface first then you can move on to explore the oceans and lakes afterwards. Get your biologists to start mapping the genes of all the species of flora and fauna as soon as possible. This information is going to be critical for your spies, tax departments and your logisticians when considering your next adventure.

19.3 Reliance. You need to find one thing that the new planet needs badly but can't provide itself. Preferably something important like water or toilet paper. If not, make sure something else becomes essential for people; get them hooked on tea, Viagrapharm or sugar. Any substance a person can't go without will do. When the demand is deeply ingrained within society, take direct and total control of the supply of that substance. This helps to keep people towing the line. If they know they will starve, die of thirst or never experience a healthy erection again, it becomes a lot harder to generate a ground-swell for any uprisings.

19.4 Spies. Get people actively eavesdropping and spying on government workers, family members and administrators as soon as possible. This intelligence structure should be completely independent of the planet's defense hierarchy. See chapter eleven for more details on this process.

19.5 Counter insurgency. If you have left a significant number of locals alive, they will rise up against you. How soon and how big the rebellion will be is going to depend on a few factors, including how badly you treat them, how naturally aggressive the species is and the preparations they made prior to the invasion. Their goal, as unlikely as it is, will be to make your stay on the planet as dangerous and uncomfortable as possible. The only way to stamp out an insurgency is with violence, retribution, rationing, collective punishment and tireless hunting, isolating, starving and killing civilians. A lot of warmongers treat uprisings as an enjoyable hobby while readying themselves for the next invasion elsewhere. If handled correctly, they can be a lot of fun.

20. Coping with Defeat

With rugby and football, if a team wins, everyone praises the wings and strikers but when that same team loses, it's the fullbacks and coaches who take the blame. Except in North Korea, where they send the whole team to forced-labor camps and never speak about that sport again. It's just the way it is. Think of yourself as the coach and know that blame will be apportioned to your office in the event of a defeat, no matter how unfair that may seem. After all, you were going to take all the credit for the win.

20.1 Contain and control. First thing, don't panic. Shut down all communication with your home world immediately. If and when the story of your loss reaches your people, it should be you who tells it. This is why you have your reserve units and plants, put them into action with a pre-determined code, mine was order 67, and execute every straggler and survivor from your defeated forces. Once all the witnesses have been eliminated you have several options to play with. You can simply leave, invent a story about a doomsday device or you can stall the news from coming out indefinitely while you try to pull off a win with a second attack. As long as you cut off the communication you have a myriad of options to play around with.

20.2 Pin it on the Gods. If your army has been decimated and you can't contain the news, it's important to get in front of the story. My go-to solution is this: You, as the leader, gave divinely inspired orders but your troops were weak and unworthy of following God's divine plan, which is why he intervened and washed the nation clean of the heretics. With the nation now purified, like silver in the fire, it's time to start another crusade and this time, he will surely keep true to his promises of victory.

20.3 Expiation. If the people aren't buying it, pick a general, place him on trial and then fairly and without bias find him guilty and hang him from the highest tree that afternoon. Be seen doing it. This will place you on the same side as the angry mobs. If it doesn't placate the masses further, give them more bodies until they are satisfied.

20.4 Crimea River. It's worked before. When an army is decimated due to incompetent senior officers barking ridiculous orders, the defeat can sometimes be spun into a moment of national pride. To accomplish this you will need: One charismatic spokesman, a poet, flags, some artificial means of faking tears and an inspirational soundtrack. Fold these ingredients gently on a national broadcasting system and express your sorrow and pride in the dignity the brave soldiers showed while dying. The people love this sort of stuff and it should suffice to placate the masses. Hold a ceremony, hand out flowers to children. Frontpages should use words like: heroes, boys, freedom, valiant and honor.

20.5 Regroup and try again. Why the hell not? So you were defeated. It's happened to the best emperors. Try to think of a defeat as a learning experience and adapt your tactics accordingly. Very often it makes sense to use less combat in your new invasion, shifting to orbital bombardment and nuclear cleansing instead of shooting and being shot at. Funding the second attempt will be difficult and you will need to use more dramatic means to get the money. But that's exactly why you chose to be a tyrant and not some polite socialist appeaser. Tax the people mercilessly, cancel any previous contracts and then open up discussions for new negotiations. Enslave a portion of your own people if you have to and sell them to the highest bidder. Do whatever needs to be done.

20.6 Fess up and cut your guts out. Perhaps the only noble thing to do when faced with a massive defeat, is to take accountability for the loss and nut up. I propose you consider making a humble, genuine speech on public television about your failure and then slowly and mindfully cut out your heart, intestines or central stomatogastric ganglion and then simply bleed out. This sort of apology is seldom made lightly and people tend to appreciate the gesture. This is exactly why you want to have at least one cloned, mind-hacked body-double in a stasis chamber somewhere. You don't really want to be cutting up your own intestines, it smells awful and hurts worse than giving birth. Ladies may argue this point. While your doppelgänger is obediently slicing open his wobbly bits, you should be sitting in a bar somewhere on an outer planet, disguised as a female air-hostess and cheering along with everybody else.

21. Subterfuge and You

War, according to your Sun Tzu, is deception, and on this point I concur with him. Throughout my career, I have forever held two parallel universes in my mind, two Armies, two fleets and two strategies. I had, through basic meditation, taught myself to visualize the upcoming battles and for each of them, as with everything, I did it twice. One battle was fought with my imaginary red army and another with the blue.

I would always begin with the blue force; imagining their formations, tactics and targets; understanding how they would attack and when. I would picture the fleet moving in mass; meditating until I could hear the guns, feel the mist, and even smell the rusty blood mixing with cordite from the gunfight. And then, when convinced it was a sound plan, I would issue the maps and orders to my generals who would distribute them to the sergeants.

Then I forgot everything and repeated the exercise, this time, with the red army. Starting with the current position of all assets, I would imagine the red scenario a little different. If the blue plan was to flank left and attack a camp at the crack of dawn, I would issue orders for the red team to advance that night and fall upon the camp as the enemy slept in comfort. If I had planned for blue's air support to scout out the surface and scorch swathes of the planet, I would have red target the local missile defenses instead. I would not issue the red orders until just before I wanted them executed.

Why did I do this? Because of spies, inductive reasoning and the subtle clues my own men would unwittingly reveal when readying themselves to carry out orders. Your adversary is always watching. Every step and action your forces take is being scrutinized by their psychiatrists, strategists and some pretty smart algorithms. The girl I was bedding could have been eavesdropping when I issued the blue orders to the generals. If not her, then the dust beneath my rack might have been nanited. I always assumed that the blue plan was compromised. If not from spies, then from my men themselves. If I had told the army to prepare to attack that night, the evening would have seen them donning their boots and scanning over maps of the area. They might have refueled their transports or looked in that direction through their scopes. Anything can tip off the enemy. By visualizing both scenarios, even psychics would be confused over which scenario was the truth.

Never tell your troops what you're planning, for they will prepare for it. Rather tell them lies and disappoint them, than tell the truth and see them butchered.

To understand war is to live with mendacity. Every step you take and order given will bring a reaction from the enemy. If you are weak on the left flank, appear strong by weakening it further, order every grunt to stand watch the entire night. If you are secure on the right flank, let it appear weak by hiding vehicles and ordering men to stay hidden in the tents. Build fake tanks out of canvas, spray paint your biological soldiers silver and make them walk awkwardly. There are simple, horrible ways to make men walk awkwardly. Execute a few men to convince your enemies that morale is slipping if it isn't. Throw a party and pretend to be feasting if you're starving. Lie. Make it your way of life. Lie all the time and then, just on occasion, show them the truth, but only when certain that they won't believe you.

While reviewing your human histories I came across hundreds of examples of battlefield subterfuge. Humans seem to have quite a knack for it. Of particular delight to me was the Second World War's 'blue plans.' For every major allied operation in the war, there was a second plan, a fake one, implemented solely to deceive enemy intelligence. Operation Neptune had Operation bodyguard, Lightfoot had Bertram, Boardman for Avalanche, Ferdinand, Mincemeat, San, and so it goes on. The amount of attention given to these deceptive operations was truly admirable and it was only through this meticulous attention to detail that the allies were able to pull them off so convincingly. There were fake troops, artillery units and tanks sitting in southern England like swimsuit models waiting to be photographed. Some of these were inflatable, while others were made of wood and hessian. Thousands of them.

In understanding modern warfare and how to make use of soldiers, artillery, tanks and mines, there is no better conflict to study than your Second World War's North African campaign. It has everything you could ask for, including some fine examples of subterfuge. In operation Bertram, tanks and artillery pieces were disguised to look like trucks and in other places fake artillery and tanks were built from reeds and canvass. Where the allies were weak, they appeared strong and the reverse was also true. At one point in this conflict, bogus artillery units were so in use that the British chanced a double bluff. By keeping a few regiments stationary and exposed for a full day, the Germans assumed the artillery to be fake, and were taken quite by surprise when they started shelling the Scheiße out of them.

Similarly, in the siege of Mafikeng, an Englishman by the name Robert Baden-Powell proved to be equally deceptive. He later became famous for a book about how he liked looking at boys. Which is weird to me, but I'm a guest on the planet, so never mind my opinion on the matter. But before all of that, he was the highest ranking British officer in a town called Mafikeng when the second Boer War broke out. Finding himself outnumbered five to one against the Boers, who were on their way to take the town, he turned to subterfuge to aid in his defense. You humans don't sing this man's praises nearly enough for what he did.

When Bob realized he didn't have enough barbed wire to erect fences around the town, he planted the posts without any wire and ordered everybody to act as if they were completed. His soldiers had to crawl under the imaginary fences, to give the appearance to the Boers watching them from afar. It worked and the Boers believed that the fences were real.

Baden-Powell didn't have much in the way of explosives either so he built dozens of wooden boxes, placing them all around the city. He then put all the explosives he had into one and detonated it in a public display. With that demonstration, he convinced everyone that all the boxes were loaded similarly and were, in fact, extremely lethal deterrents against an enemy attack. Of course the remaining were all empty. Again, the enemy bought it.

The town only had only gun and he drilled his units hard, moving the artillery piece around to create the impression that they had many cannons. When the real unit wasn't in place it was substituted with a tree trunk fashioned to look like a cannon from a distance.

All his deception, even though it may seem quite silly now, worked and worked well. It helped him to keep the enemy at bay for seven months and Baden-Powell returned home as a hero and was made the youngest lieutenant-general of the British army. Whoever said lying and cheating doesn't pay off, never pulled on a pair of combat boots.

22. Survival Strategies for a Burgeoning Civilization

22.1 The numbers. The Nebraxian poem entitled: "Greetings. Is it me you're searching for?" is their equivalent to your drake equation, only infinitely more eloquent and moving. Nebraxian poetry is written with two similar stanzas designed to be read simultaneously. One stanza for each hemisphere of the brain. By reading this way, it can highlight similarities and divergences of ideas. Of course, very few humans can read like this but you should try. Ginsberg once came close to capturing this effect when he kept referring back to Rockland. This is the best Earthlish translation I could manage:

The cosmos wills a star into being. This	*The cosmos wills a star into being. This*
star throws a planet before it at arm's	*star throws a planet before it at arm's*
length, to enjoy a mild warmth. The	*length, to enjoy a mild warmth. The*
youngster takes to spinning around	*youngster takes to spinning around*
itself and around the star in a steady	*itself and around the star in a steady*
dance. Life blooms. The blooming,	*dance. Life blooms. The blooming,*
learns to think, the thinking sings out,	*learns to think, the thinking sings out,*
the song is carried through the abyss at	*the song is carried through the abyss at*
1420.4 MHz. This voice is heard by	*1420.4 MHz. This voice is heard by*
others. Those with ears listen. A reply is	*others. Those with ears listen. Those*
constructed, and those with ears build	*with ears ready their armies and set out*
themselves a voice, reply and together	*to extinguish the destroyers of the*
they sing a duet through the ages.	*divine silence, and take their planets*
Advancing their civilisations in unison	*and peoples for their troubles.*

Figure 18. Nebraxian Drake

In chapter five, we spoke about your Drake equation but I only told you half the story. You need to be aware that while you are out looking for rich, weakly defended planets to colonize, annex or strip mine, so is everybody else in the universe. Real estate is the only game in the universe and it's always a conquering tyrants market.

The universe is roughly 14 billion years old. Let's assume an advanced civilization can survive for 5,000 years, measured from when they first invent a means to broadcast radio waves, until the time they die out due to genetic degradation, a fatal STD, annihilation or simple boredom. 5,000 years is immensely generous in my experience. After all, your species has only been 'advanced' for less than 150 years. And do even you expect to make another two centuries? You do? How Quaint. You won't.

With that in mind, the likelihood that a species is mature and alive right now, as opposed to any other point in time, is therefore roughly one in three million.

Another aspect Drake overlooked, is the likelihood of the second civilization being capable of annihilating you. If we assume that 5,000 years is accurate, the chances of your civilization being older, and therefore more technologically advanced, is roughly your age divided by 5,000. Obviously, assuming both societies progress at a similar rate.

To express this in Earthlish:

$fo = fa / L$

fo = *the likelihood of your civilisation being more mature than a second one.*

fa = *The advanced age of your civilization in years.*

L = *The length of time which civilizations release detectable signals into space.*

Figure 19. Likelihood of being technologically advanced.

So for Earth today, the chances of you being more advance than a second species is roughly three percent. Unless you're a gambling man, now might not be the right time to be out searching among the stars.

But what is the likelihood of any extra-terrestrial civilization you encounter being hostile? In Nebraxian, this variable is simply stated as 'yes,' and in Earthlish, in my experience it should be represented as one and therefore doesn't need its own variable but in the interest of fairness and accuracy I have included it into the formula as fh. And for the purposes of optimism, let's assume that only three out of four creatures you encounter will want to kill you.

$$Certain\ Death = (1\text{-}fo)\ x\ fh$$

Figure 20. Equation for Certain Death

So for Earth right now, any unannounced guest would be bringing a 73 percent chance of certain death with their arrival, though, to be fair, your new friends might just choose to enslave your kind. That will still result in the demise of your civilization, it's just a slower, nastier way to exit the universe.

Your scientists will argue that although a civilization might be able to hear your radio waves, they might not be able to get to Earth. Pish tosh, I say unto them, but fine, have a variable, call it *ft*, and let's say it's a 50:50 chance, if that will help you to sleep at night. That's a fifty percent chance that any species hearing your radios are capable of FTL or space-time folding.

I've taken the liberty of making a couple of additions to Drake's awkward prose, to incorporate the above variables we have just discussed.

$E = R^* \times f_p \times n_e \times f_l \times f_i \times f_c \times f_s \times L \times (1-fo) \times fh \times ft$

Where:

E = # civilisations in the Milky Way right now, who want to, and can kill you.

R· = the rate in which stars are formed in your galaxy

f_p = the likelihood of a star holding stable planets within its gravity

n_e = the likelihood of one having an environment capable of sustaining life

f_l = The likelihood of those planets that can support life actually doing so.

f_i = The chance of that life advancing to intelligent life.

f_c = The chance of that intelligent life being capable of radio communication.

L = The length of time those civilizations release detectable signals into space

fo = the likelihood of your civilisation being more mature than a second one.

ft = the likelihood of a nation capable of fast interstellar travel

fa = The advanced age of your civilization in years

fh = The likelihood a civilization is hostile.

Figure 21. Updated Drake Equation

Drake's original set of variables gave him an optimistic answer of 100 million civilizations in the universe. With our additions to his original set, we can now safely say that of those 100 million, 36 million are capable of ending all life on earth and are actively trying to. Do you still believe it wise to be broadcasting your position into the gaping maw of space and eternity?

In light of the above, I know you want to get into the darkness and start conquering, but you must always be aware of others like you, with better technology and larger armies, who too are hunting planets. So regardless of your conquests and success rate, your civilization remains at risk of a random encounter with an empire who will render your flesh for profit. There are four strategies employed to mitigate the chance of this occurring: Taste bad, run fast, fight well or hide. These four strategies or combinations thereof are the only permanent options for survival in this harsh universe. Some species have placed their hopes in silly attributes like intelligence, charisma, usefulness or even deities but without exception, those nations have either been removed from the playing field or adapted their strategies quickly. If you aren't running, hiding, fighting or repulsing, you are on a path which can only end in annihilation.

So often, intelligent, funny and docile nations have slept easily, relying on contracts or non-aggression treaties to protect them, while on some nearby moon their enemies go about hurriedly assembling legions of death-robots and deploying nano-ninjas into key positions.

We all live in a dark and desolate combat zone. The very space around us tends towards chaos, to madness and destruction, and to think otherwise is to be ignorant of the nature of the universe. It is that sort of thinking that will leave your civilization a collection of bones and ruins, for future aliens to kick over ponderously.

22.2 Tasting Bad. Some species are born tasting bad but for those less fortunate, there are many ways to achieve inedibility. Your scientists should be able to help with this. Sometimes it's as simple as altering your people's diet or introducing toxic substances into your atmosphere. On other occasions it may require genetic manipulation or even surgery. The benefits to this strategy should be obvious. Most invasions take place because of the invaders desire to eat your people and resources so, by making these inedible, it defeats their reason for war.

Many robotic and ethereal nations in the universe today are so formed as a result of their quest to offer their enemies no suste-nance in defeat. The tasting bad strategy deals with more than your own bodies though, your abodes need to appear uncomfortable to the enemy, you should have no apparent resources visible, your technology should be antiquated and your females must be hideous. Hideous.

Some people have stated that the tasting bad strategy is in fact worse than the genocide it is meant to prevent. Those people have yet to witness a neutronic cull ship working through their neighborhood, while it's approaching the local kindergarten.

Tasting bad is, however, no protection against genocidal tyrants who are looking for a war. If a true warmonger discovers your planet, he may decide to invade or nuke the planet from orbit anyway. Out of spite. As I might. That will depend on the nature of the warmonger, the distance to the planet and subsequent logistics costs to invade or destroy. The drawback is this, if 'tasting bad' has been implemented well, you will probably lack the resources to fight back effectively. This strategy was used by the Scottish against the English, Romans and the Vikings. Even to this day the Scots taste terrible.

22.3 Running fast is a useful strategy when you encounter a superior force you have no chance of defeating in open combat. Generally, full populations can't be taken off planet so a choice needs to be made. Some societies have opted for lotteries to select which individuals get seats on the carriers. The Gentriac nation, before embarking on their great trek, selected males according to their skillsets and females according to their attractiveness.

Once the decision has been made it's important to start building as many carriers as possible. Get long-range scouts and telescopes out, looking for planets capable of sustaining life. Develop resource maps to understand what is available and where, and disseminate the information to all vessels in the fleet. When running fast, build lots of small and medium sized ships instead of a few behemoths. Build utility ships instead of working their functionality into other vessels. This way, it allows for sharing and reduces wasting resources on redundant devices. Generally, air scrubbing, filtering, water recycling and maintenance should be built into stand-alone, dedicated vessels. When drives or life support systems fail, plans can be made. Send several small fleets instead of one large one, the enemy will probably be out looking for you. It's a good idea to settle into a nomadic lifestyle, instead of harboring any hope of finding a lovely green, wet planet with a similar gravity to which you are accustomed. Chances are, if a planet like that does exist, it will be inhabited by people more capable of holding it than you are of taking it. Running fast was used by the Scythians, Native Americans and less effectively, the French.

22.4 Fighting well. Most of this book is dedicated to the science of fighting. In particular we have focused on how to select and invade an unsuspecting planet. In the next chapter we will look at that same sort of war from the other side. Remember, before engaging in conflict with a new species, one should also consider the temperament, technology, allies and abilities of the species in question. If choosing to opt for violence, it is preferable that you are a warrior nation, enjoying the top of the food chain, with a history of violence and aggression. If not, if you consist of a diet of fungi and non-sentient vegetable matter, war will probably not come easy to you. Fighting well was employed by the Zulus, the Mongolians and Sparta.

22.5 Hiding. Some planets right now are actively sending radio-waves, light and signals out into the universe. Several of these signals are not even disguised to hide any discernible patterns. Of course, these planets will all be picked clean in a matter of time. In all cases history has taught us that these signals are either a form of mass suicide or the result of ignorance of the highest order. Your planet should be giving off absolutely no signals. If capable, you should be negating the effects of gravity from your entire solar system. Make use of nebula's or wormholes if possible. What you want is for your system to look like a nondescript section of space, without any reason for inquisitive warmongers to investigate.

One problem with hiding is the Reticulan species. These beings are the most prolific explorers in the known universe. They are short, frail, bipeds with large eyes and clammy grey skin, with short-range telepathic abilities. They've been at it for several hundred thousand millennia, so they might very well have recorded your planet or even seeded it to suit their victualing needs. If this is the case, you should know Reticulan reports are bouncing around in the universe and the most advance species have learned to record and file these reports. If your planet is described in one of those, you're screwed. The good news is the Reticulans have only travelled and documented around four percent of the universe. Hiding was used by the Welsh against the Vikings.

23. Leading an Insurgency

An amateur astronomer is going to notice the absence of a star. The sort of people who regularly look at the night sky tend to be humble and rational, and that's why he's going to doubt himself and phone a friend, who will confirm it is indeed missing. By the time an official piece of glass is aimed at the space, everything will be back to normal and the event will be scratched up to human error.

Over the course of three or four weeks, a few dozen people are going to go missing, in seemingly random, rural locations around the planet, but you won't notice this. One or two stories might make the tabloids, talking about probes and bright lights but you will disregard their accounts as fictitious, sad calls for attention.

An ongoing gravity survey in the South Pacific might pick up an anomalous result, but when the scan is conducted a second time, it will read 9.81 meters per second as expected.

Without anyone being aware of it, thousands of inert metallic rods will be positioned in decaying orbits by drones high above the planet. They're going to be abandoned there, subject only to basic mechanics, most importantly, gravity. Their descent will take a week or so, but their impact with the surface has just become the starter gun.

On Earth, life will carry on. Your people will go about their days, scratching out their little lives, unaware that their fate has already been decided by forces beyond their ken.

About eight minutes and twenty seconds before the first rod's impact, a Z-class solar flare is going to erupt in what was previously considered to be a calm section of your sun. The initial effects of the flare will be nothing more than a pretty light show. That will change when the ensuing EMP pulse turns off your broadcast signals and electrical devices. All cell phones, computers and radios will go dark at this point and most vehicles built in the last two decades will be rendered inoperable. Later still, power grids will overload and transformers all across the planet will turn into massive pyres stretching into the night's sky.

Australis and Borealis will meet for the first time in millennia above the equator, offering light sufficient to read by. As that is happening, those metallic rods will begin hitting missile silos, communications systems and any bases with a classification of FB or higher, probably your throne room and your official residence too.

Your surviving presidents, generals and admirals, cut off from communication networks, won't know if the Earth is under attack or merely victim of some solar weather phenomenon. If they somehow have been notified of the recent systematic destruction of so many military installations, they might assume the attack to be terrestrial in nature and target old enemies out of habit. Some will try to launch retaliatory strikes and a few might even succeed. It's irrelevant. Even if they knew it to be an alien attack they would have nothing to target their remaining systems on.

The enemy will not come. They will remain in hiding, waiting for the storm to pass on the lee side of the moon. They will watch with curiosity as your proud armies succumb to burning and terror, your cities falling dark, one after the other, your citizens running amok in the streets, others calling out to neglected deities who are no longer listening.

And still, the enemy will not come. Days will pass like this. Humans will make runs for food, water and for shelter; killing one another, much to the amusement of the watching aliens. Rumors and myths will pass between your people as they did in the old days. Monsters and demons with forgotten names will emerge to lurk in the dark corners of your rooms, just outside of the candlelight. When sleep comes, it will be fraught with nightmares and not even the occasional gunfire from your neighbors will suffice to wake you from those horrors. And still the enemy will not come.

Four days, I would estimate. Four days, while they hunker down to avoid the worst of the storm of their own making. Only once it's completely dissipated will they break formation and abandon the protection of the dusty moon craters.

Then they will come, in overwhelming numbers and with weapons unimaginable. Troops, vehicles, crawling things and robots, all descending in mass, while orbital ion cannons or something similar begins to lay waste to your remaining defenses. Efficiently, they will come to silence your kind forever. No one they catch will be spared, your children will be treated like you treat lambs. The elderly, wealthy and culturally interesting will taste just as good as simple industrial workers. The faithless and faithful will be measured only by their body masses. All will be deemed worthy of the meat factories and their ever-spinning grinders.

This isn't the war you wanted but here it is. In the parlance of the day: It sucks to be you, now nut up and start your insurgency.

23.1 Preparation. If you're ever going to survive an invasion, you need to assume the enemy is on the way right now and prepare for them before they arrive. Yes, the costs will be substantial and hopefully this investment will never be needed. But do it anyway. Don't wait for signs, by then it will be too late.

You need to develop and distribute an evacuation plan, to get yourself and the people you will need safely out of the cities. Purchase and cache weapons and supplies all around the world, in hidden bunkers and subsurface facilities. Assume that all of your military and police services will be compromised or destroyed during the invasion and establish a second structure now. Work with this militia and treat them as a clandestine security group. If you have the money, take a central airport, say Denver for example, and rebuild it so it can withstand direct ballistic hits of massive payloads. Build it to be capable of housing thousands of troops, deep beneath the surface. Stock it with food, beverages, weapons and ammunitions. Try to keep it secret. A central, easy-to-access hub like this will become your new headquarters when the aliens land. Without these preparations, there will probably still be an insurrection, it just won't be you leading it and it will likely end a lot sooner.

23.2 Soldiers. With your military in tatters, you should expect very little help from standing regular forces but there are other people available. Reservists and veterans should make up the bulk of your initial militia. As time passes, with your men out on patrols, you will find civilians who are capable of joining and supporting your army.

In the cities, keep an eye out for ex-cops, gang members and bouncers with foreign military training, especially Russians. Dentists and guidance counselors make excellent suicide bombers. Pull in engineers, mechanics, electricians and doctors as a priority, you're going to need them.

In rural areas, reach out to hunters, gun-nuts, end of the world lunatics and any other sort of inbred, half-bearded, cousin-fucking hicks who are willing. They all tend to have excellent survival, hunting and tracking skills and will make great recon units and irregulars.

23.3 The goal of an insurgency is simple. You want to make life so uncomfortable for your new masters that they choose to leave for greener pastures. This can be done by cutting off their food supplies, poisoning their water sources, destroying their fuel, irradiating their iridium and minerals, or killing a large percentage of the invaders themselves, preferably painfully. They have to lose their taste for the planet. Every step they take should be fraught with danger from landmines and IEDs. Every time they see your blue skies, they should be looking expectantly for the tell-tale glint of a sniper's scope in the distance. If they pass a bowel movement, they should wonder if your forces are about to introduce some intestinal parasite into their system. Every breath – a possible threat from a weaponized spore or virus. Whores with the death-clap: doors with booby-traps: food with salmonella: hints of almond in the tea. Only after years of constant fear and discomfort will an alien nation consider leaving.

23.4 Go underground. Not metaphorically. Physically underground, preferably deep. Underground has been the go-to base location ever since Americans started invading countries for entertainment. With alien technology sweeping the landscape, searching for terrorists, it's going to be your best choice too. The problem with living underground is it tends to be dark, cold, and aside from mushrooms, it provides no sustenance. Hopefully you've stocked a few bunkers around the planet full with K rations and weapons. Bases should have fresh-water sources, springs and aquifers wherever possible and they all need to have generators to provide electricity and appropriate ventilation, to prevent the exhaust fumes from killing all your soldiers on a calm evening.

In cities, look to sewers and drainage systems, use buildings only if they are long-abandoned and offer multiple escape routes. Underground railways, tube stations and bunkers should all be mapped, reviewed and kept secret from all but those who reside in them.

In rural areas, look for mineshafts, caves, tunnels or bunkers. Any structures that will provide shelter, escape and a modicum of comfort should be utilized. Try to use them for a while and then move on at irregular intervals. If possible, set up mines and tripwires to give you a few minutes warning of an impending attack. Deploy dogs at entrances, to identify robots masquerading as humans speaking English with Austrian accents.

23.5 Stealth. Your previous army had shiny insignia and vehicles. They drove around in daylight with impunity. They fucking played bugles every evening. You won't be doing any of that anymore. Now your men will be walking softy in the woods on the night of the dead moon. If daylight finds them above ground, they need to hunker down, dig in, and pretend to be shrubbery for the next twelve hours. You get Scottish suits that can help you do this. Practice helps, so will the older reservists who have served in jungles.

Depending on your foes abilities, you will need to learn how to mask the signs of your passing. This may involve using spices, placed on the ground to damage the noses of bloodhounds, explosives work too, or using the ancient, Native American ploys of erasing your tracks behind you, by drag branches.

23.6 Small cells. You want to have many small units working and living independently. Large armies are going to be discovered and neutralized quickly. Small independent cells will allow you to spread out across a larger playing field. Everyone should be actively watching the enemy and reporting it to a central structure. Hunting will also become an important activity and by spreading out you won't be decimating the local wildlife in one area.

23.7 Local support. As with all guerrilla wars, you need to quickly establish a network of locals who aren't militant but are willing to support you. They will prove crucial in the war effort, helping to spy for you and supply your men with any food they can spare. They will do so at great risk to themselves, if they believe in the cause. Be careful, if they are taken in for questioning, especially if they have children, they will compromise your position very quickly when tortured. So it is best that you treat them like you would a clingy sexual partner, always going to visit them and never letting them know where you live. The less they know, the safer it is for everyone. If you suspect they have been compromised, kill them and relocate. Again, like you would a clingy sexual partner.

23.8 Living off the enemy. You have to learn how to use your adversary's weapons as soon as possible. Your rifles are more than likely going to prove inadequate and even if not, your ammunition caches will deplete rapidly while you're engaging in regular skirmishes. Capturing live aliens has to be a top priority, interrogate them to learn their military structures, plans and placement. Try to learn their language if it's physically possible. Learn how to use their weapons and equipment and then modify them to better suit your soldiers. Continue to watch and study their movements and tactics, until you find patterns you can use against them.

23.9 Communications. All those clever inventions of yours, your beloved cell phones, land lines, computers, radios and telegraphs are done. All of these can and will be detected, your location will be triangulated, bringing the invaders to your door. You're going to need a network of runners. Nobody is going to want to be one, because of all the running involved, and the increased likelihood of winding up on an alien captain's dinner table doesn't help. You're going to need to encourage these people with stories of glory and importance. Generally teenage boys are your go-to choice. Be careful. If an experienced runner is ever captured and interrogated, he will know all your locations in an area, along with a lot of the intelligence regarding the local military structures. Wherever possible try to limit his knowledge by having him meet other runners at set points, rather than running from base to base. This way, no runner will know more than one or two locations. Have them run with written, encrypted notes, to keep them ignorant of the intelligence they are carrying. Burn all communiques once read.

23.10 Choose your targets. Once your militia is established, you need to start making it uncomfortable for the enemy. Your primary targets should be logistics supplies, fuel dumps and high ranking enemy officers. How and when you attack should be random, which isn't as easy as you would imagine. Try to vary your methods, frequency and targets to keep the enemy awake at night and worried about their assets, loved ones and arses. Your first choice is to steal resources before destroying them. It's a lot harder to pull off but it's equally more rewarding.

23.11 Insurgency tactics. I've been on the other side of an insurgency before, as an invader, I can tell you, it can be frustrating. The terrorists seem to have all the advantages. They decide when and where to attack and they disappear as quickly as they came. Poorer countries tend to fare better than wealthier ones, simply because the soldiers are conditioned to going with less. They know their own country because they have walked it, while hunting and travelling. For example, Yemen is going to hold out a lot longer than America or Germany. If possible, try to get to one of these countries and start up from there.

24. The Inevitable Outcome

You are going to die. Yes, even you. It's going come as a surprise. Death isn't going to wait for you to complete your rampage or dispatch all of your enemies. The Nebraxian Poet, Neville, said it best: "I must fear. For fear alone clears the mind. I will let it envelop me. Fear will show me my enemies approach so I may prepare my defenses against them. Everyone, even aspects of my own self, stand against me. I will strike them down before they can act. I will know peace in the grave and not before. I must fear everyone and everything for they are plotting, in the dark corners. Assassins wear the faces of my family. It is only through fear that I can hear them whispering to one another, colluding in the shadows. If I trust no one, I can never be betrayed."

That poem was my mantra for so many years, helping to keep my mind aware of the challenges of the throne; those imminent dangers lurking at every moment. Even now, on Earth, and no longer in power, I still return to this poem daily and let it refresh my paranoia. I would encourage any warmonger to do the same.

The science of death, thanatology, is one of the least understood of all the scientific disciplines but we know that death comes in three flavors:

24.1 A Natural death. Your heart will start losing time with that electric metronome built into your body, that you haven't noticed before. Your mind becomes aware of the shift in the rhythm, panics, and frantically starts pumping adrenaline into your bloodstream, in a futile attempt to prolong your suffering. It doesn't help. Not this time. Slowly, the world is pulled from you. Pulled from you like a child clutching a possession that he'd taken hold of, but was never his to begin with. The world pulls back further still and the sounds of life are muffled to silence, and then you find yourself looking into a familiar emptiness. You realize that it's okay, while a kind warmth envelops your naked self. There's nothing to be proud or shameful of here. You notice your body, now without substance, feeling natural, freed from all that heavy flesh you've been carrying for so long. For just a moment, you consider panicking, then you forget to.

There's no need to protect yourself. You're not unique. You know it. You have no secrets in need of keeping anymore. There's even less weight to you. You search yourself and realize you own no memories so important that they can't be shrugged from your shoulders and as you do, you're instantly as light as hydrogen. Now you're transitioning from being no-one, to being nothing. It's like drawing air again after a lifetime of suffocating. At this point in the process, some of the more stubborn among us look back at the place they just left, and each and every one whispers only this: "What a weird little place that was."

And then there is nothing.

24.2 A Quick death. A gunshot rings out while you're orating to a crowd of adoring underlings. A sharp impact to your back wakes you in the middle of the night and you smell iron in the air and wonder: Why am I wet? Standing in an assembly, debating with your peers, a few men close in on you and you notice the flash of a dagger and feel something pulling at your belly. A small team of uniformed soldiers aim their weapons at your chest, then a senior officer orders them to take aim, and then fire, and then they do. A parachute doesn't open, even while scrambling for the backup, you already know that it won't work either. One evening, your wine tastes a little different, is that almonds? In your robotic body, someone sets your new batteries to explode and your CPU is damaged beyond repair. But most likely, for you, your quick death will come from loved ones, probably friends and family, kicking you to death outside of a pub, in a street or a city named after you.

And then there is nothing.

24.3 A painful death. Someone has set you on fire, has you on a rack, or is conducting a fastidious dissection on your body. They've removed your poison tooth and over-ridden your mind's control of your heartbeat. You're bleeding out slowly. The only difference between this method and the others is the screaming. If you need consolation, think of this: You've done a few of these sorts of executions in your time and every one was far more expertly administered than the one these weak-willed, shaky-handed pussies are clumsily attempting.

And then there is nothing.

24.4 Avoiding a natural death

24.4.1 Personal fitness. Being fit will make you better looking, increase you lifespan, help your martial arts, improve your mental acuity, amplify your psychic abilities, earn the respect of your soldiers, intimidate your enemies, improve your lovemaking skills, reduce your logistics requirements, and double your chances of conceiving an heir. On the down side it will take up an hour every day, which you could spend watching reality TV and / or masturbating. Your decision.

24.4.2 Doctors. Getting full check-ups quarterly will help to reduce your insurance premiums and perhaps allow you to prevent an unnecessary death which could have been avoided through medicine or surgery. For your best results, link your doctor's well-being to your own and insist he be buried beside you, regardless of the cause.

24.4.3 Backups. Consider clones, brain transplants or having your mind digitized and stored for safekeeping. But know that all of these solutions are only temporary measures. Hard-drives corrupt, clones get diseases, and all of your fail-safes will be prime targets for any usurper to your throne.

24.5 Avoiding a Quick Death

24.5.1 Self-defense. Study boxing or another practical and aggressive form of martial arts – not a sport derived from a training method for combat. Learn how to throw a punch and take one too. Carry at least three small, concealed weapons at all times, one of which should be a pistol or ray gun. Your sensei or sifu will only take you so far, they are legally bound to prevent you from mastering the crippling and killing techniques. So you will have to master these on your own. Begin your training outside junior schools, then slowly move on to old age homes, then grocery aisles and finally alleyways outside of bars.

While hand to hand combat is useful, it's no match for a side arm. While studying the martial arts, you should also be training in parallel in combat shooting, under a proficient marksman. This will also come in handy when your martial training goes wrong in the supermarket and you need to get out quickly and reconsider your techniques. There's no shame in bugging out of a fight with a ten-year-old by shooting the assailant and legging it.

24.5.2 Home / Office defense. Sleep with motion detectors linked to alarms within the room. Ensure your sleeping chamber is completely sealed and without any light sources. Pitch darkness will help you to see better than your enemies can. If they come equipped with night vision goggles, you can use one of the flash bangs you keep under your pillow to disorientate them and gain the upper hand. I like to have a couple of small, nervous dogs at the foot of my bed as they will wake you to any unexpected sounds or smells. Regular, random beatings will keep them nervous. Obviously you will want a small arsenal of modern weaponry close at hand. Have your air conditioners fitted with particle detectors and have an air supply stored in sealed tanks for emergencies. Monitor who your guardsmen speak to and sleep with if they aren't gelded. Don't have any Wi-

Fi connections if you have robotic housekeepers or guards, as they could be hacked and be reprogrammed to kill you. Equip your house with anti-drone weaponry on your rooftop. Tin foil night caps will keep psychics out of your nightmares. If possible, try to build your living-quarters at least four stories beneath the surface, encased in alternating layers of reinforced concrete and steel plating. You should have electromagnetic pads around all apertures to catch any nanites trying to sneak in.

24.5.3 Diet. Stick to the four standard meals you can prepare yourself or visit a warehouse once in a while and handpick a crate of rations at random. Personally supervise the meals being loaded and placed in your locked bedroom. Do the same for water, prophylactics, coffee beans and toothpaste.

24.5.4 Hygiene. Never wear the same clothing twice as poison can be introduced into your skin through fabric. Have your body doubles do all the baby kissing, handshaking and work the rope lines for you. Pick your love interests in a similar manner to the way you secure your rations. Never sleep with the same female twice. Any woman who initiates a second round with you must be a masochist or a spy, either way it's best to avoid her or treat her as a double agent.

24.5.5 Meetings / Restaurants. Always sit facing the door, regardless of the number of secret service members you have surrounding you. Make sure they search everyone for weapons whenever they approach you, even if they just left the table to go to the bathroom. Often assassins will go to the bathroom to retrieve a taped pistol, earlier stashed behind the cistern.

24.5.6 Transport protocols. The reason why animals don't follow steady patterns is it's dangerous. A frog croaking at regular intervals will allow a predator to locate it in the dark. Buck going to the same drinking hole at the same time every day would soon be ambushed by lions. Learn from Mother Nature and do not follow patterns. Take a different route to work every day, send dummy convoys on alternate routes and vary your positioning within the real convoy of identical cars, obviously never the first vehicle.

24.5.7 Monologuing. Don't gloat over the dying bodies of your enemies, unless they have been checked for poisonous teeth and hidden explosives first. Never break into monologues about how you outsmarted someone until you've shot them in the head first. If you have to brag, have their heads reanimated and talk to them then.

24.5.8 Public engagements. Avoid driving in open-topped cars or walking through exposed areas without coverings placed to obscure sniper fire, regardless of how lovely the weather is or how adored you are by the masses.

24.5.9 Deterrents. Make the punishment for regicide the most painful, horrific means of execution you can imagine. Let the punishment be carried out not just on the assassin but on the family and friends of the transgressor as a further deterrent. Make sure everyone understands the penalty for such a heinous crime. The executions should be broadcast on national TV and betting on the side should be encouraged. Anyone complaining about the barbarity of the act clearly doesn't hold your life in high regard, consider something similar for these detractors.

24.6 Avoiding a painful death. The only guaranteed method to avoid a painful death would be to not anger anyone to the point where they will want to torture and kill you. So, clearly not an option for you.

24.6.1 Watch lists. Because of the nature of betrayal, your would-be usurper will never be someone you suspect. For this reason I strongly recommend you outsource the development of the watch-list, to two individuals who are impartial and equally paranoid. Kill the person who returns the shorter list, along with the people whose names are absent. The missing names are probably the short comer's co-conspirators.

Conducting monthly purges of people in positions of power also helps. If you have no actionable intelligence that month, take one or two people out at random; they won't know what you know. Torture them – you might be pleasantly surprised by what they tell you. Some of it might even be true. In Communist Russia, members of the politburo were 'invited' to stay in a nearby secure building. When they fell out of favour with Stalin, he made use of the hidden tunnels and entrances to steal their families away in the middle of the night, without anyone noticing their disappearances and murders. Ruthless, clean, efficient and terrifying. Sure, rumors of the tunnels surfaced, but how well would you sleep that night if you had voiced your opinion against the man of steel earlier that day?

Conclusion

This isn't all I know about the important arts and sciences but it is all I'm willing to share, here, now, with the likes of you.

Take what's been said and think on these things, then decide for yourself if they have value. Find your own truth or forever allow yourself to be deceived by others.

My hope for you is that one day, you will rise up and be counted as the champion of Earth and a worthy nemesis; a true leader, unashamed to take the title of emperor and wear that mantle proudly. For your current controllers are cowardly, miserly men who take the wealth from others and then do nothing with it. Each one, mortal. Each one, clutching and forever counting. Each fearing that what they found by chance will be taken by someone more deserving.

Above all things, I have longed for this: One last adversary to stand against. That I might engage in open combat with a worthy challenger again. That I might find the will to summon up the blood and don my armor one last time. And there, on a green field of my choosing, watch my final battle unfold. Soldiers screaming for vocals, Stalin on the organs, artillery beating the earth like a base drum. All of it scented with a heady, sweet napalm. And I in the thick of it, hands raw from wrenching lives asunder, throat dry from the shouting of orders, legs growing weak but still stepping over the fallen. In the quiet moments, listening for mothers wailing in despair at the sight of their fallen sons. Is that too much to ask for?

And there you can pitch your men against my minions and we can see how they fare. I will show you more about the arts of war on that day. I will show you wonders you haven't the mental capacity to imagine. Terrifying, frenzying, splendid things, which will leave your mouth agape and your men trembling as my horrors lurch towards them hungrily.

And if I were to fall on that day, what a prize you shall have! If I were to find the ground holding me at last; in that embrace I will tell you all the secrets of the universe known to me and they are legion. Then, finally, I would pass into the screaming well of darkness; content with a life well-fought. You can look down on my bloodless corpse, scan up across the lands you can now call yours, and then higher still. Looking up at the night sky, you can pick a star, point to it and say this: "There, that is where we begin."

COSMIC
EGG
BOOKS

If you prefer to spend your nights with Vampires and
Werewolves rather than the mundane then we publish the books
for you. If your preference is for Dragons and Faeries or Angels
and Demons – we should be your first stop. Perhaps your
perfect partner has artificial skin or comes from another planet –
step right this way. Our curiosity shop contains treasures you
will enjoy unearthing. If your passion is Fantasy (including
magical realism and spiritual fantasy), Horror or Science Fiction
(including Steampunk), Cosmic Egg books will
feed your hunger.